P9-ELQ-530

THE GHOST NEXT DOOR

THE GHOST NEXT DOOR

R.L. STINE

SCHOLASTIC INC.
New York Toronto London Auckland Sydney
Mexico City New Delhi Hong Kong Buenos Aires

ISBN 0-439-56832-3

12 11 10   5 6 7 8/0

Printed in the U.S.A.   40

First Scholastic printing, August 1993

Hannah wasn't sure which had awakened her — the brittle crackling sounds or the bright yellow flames.

She sat straight up in bed and stared in wide-eyed horror at the fire that surrounded her.

Flames rippled across her dresser. The burning wallpaper curled and then melted. The door of her closet had burned away, and she could see the fire leaping from shelf to shelf.

Even the mirror was on fire. Hannah could see her reflection, dark behind the wall of flickering flames.

The fire moved quickly to fill the room.

Hannah began to choke on the thick, sour smoke.

It was too late to scream.

But she screamed anyway.

* * *

How nice to find out it was only a dream.

Hannah sat up in bed, her heart pounding, her mouth as dry as cotton.

No crackling flames. No leaping swirls of yellow and orange.

No choking smoke.

All a dream, a horrible dream. So real.

But a dream.

"Wow. That was really scary," Hannah muttered to herself. She sank back on her pillow and waited for her heart to stop thudding so hard in her chest. She raised her gray-blue eyes to the ceiling, staring at the cool whiteness of it.

Hannah could still picture the black, charred ceiling, the curling wallpaper, the flames tossing in front of the mirror.

"At least my dreams aren't *boring*!" she told herself. Kicking off the light blanket, she glanced at her desk clock. Only eight-fifteen.

How can it only be eight-fifteen? she wondered. I feel as if I've been sleeping forever. What day is it, anyway?

It was hard to keep track of these summer days. One seemed to melt into another.

Hannah was having a lonely summer. Most of her friends had gone away on family vacations or to camp.

There was so little for a twelve-year-old to do in a small town like Greenwood Falls. She read a lot of books and watched a lot of TV and rode her bike around town, looking for someone to hang out with.

Boring.

But today Hannah climbed out of bed with a smile on her face.

She was alive!

Her house hadn't burned down. She hadn't been trapped inside the crackling wall of flames.

Hannah pulled on a pair of Day-Glo green shorts and a bright orange sleeveless top. Her parents were always teasing her about being color blind.

"Give me a *break*! What's the big deal if I like bright colors?" she always replied.

Bright colors. Like the flames around her bed.

"Hey, dream — get *lost*!" she muttered. She ran a hairbrush quickly through her short blonde hair, then headed down the hall to the kitchen. She could smell the eggs and bacon frying on the stove.

"Good morning, everyone!" Hannah chirped happily.

She was even happy to see Bill and Herb, her six-year-old twin brothers.

Pests. The noisiest nuisances in Greenwood Falls.

They were tossing a blue rubber ball across the breakfast table. "How many times do I have to tell you — no ball-playing in the house?" Mrs. Fairchild called, turning away from the stove to scold them.

"A million," Bill said.

Herb laughed. He thought Bill was hilarious. They both thought they were a riot.

Hannah stepped behind her mother and wrapped her up in a tight hug around the waist.

"Hannah — stop!" her mother cried. "I nearly knocked over the eggs!"

"Hannah — stop! Hannah — stop!" The twins imitated their mother.

The ball bounced off Herb's plate, rebounded off the wall, and flew onto the stove, inches from the frying pan.

"Nice shot, ace," Hannah teased.

The twins laughed their high-pitched laughs.

Mrs. Fairchild spun around, frowning. "If the ball goes in the frying pan, you're going to *eat* it with your eggs!" she threatened, shaking her fork at them.

This made the boys laugh even harder.

"They're in goofy moods today," Hannah said, smiling. She had a dimple in one cheek when she smiled.

"When are they ever in *serious* moods?" her mother demanded, tossing the ball into the hallway.

"Well, I'm in a *great* mood today!" Hannah declared, gazing out the window at a cloudless, blue sky.

Her mother stared at her suspiciously. "How come?"

4

Hannah shrugged. "I just am." She didn't feel like telling her mother about the nightmare, about how good it felt just to be alive. "Where's Dad?"

"Went to work early," Mrs. Fairchild said, turning the bacon with the fork. "Some of us don't get the entire summer off," she added. "What are you going to do today, Hannah?"

Hannah opened the refrigerator and pulled out a carton of orange juice. "The usual, I guess. You know. Just hang out."

"I'm sorry you're having such a boring summer," her mother said, sighing. "We just didn't have the money to send you to camp. Maybe next summer — "

"That's okay, Mom," Hannah replied brightly. "I'm having an okay summer. Really." She turned to the twins. "How'd you guys like those ghost stories last night?"

"Not scary," Herb quickly replied.

"Not scary at all. Your ghost stories are dumb," Bill added.

"You guys looked pretty scared to me," Hannah insisted.

"We were pretending," Herb said.

She held up the orange juice carton. "Want some?"

"Does it have pulp in it?" Herb asked.

Hannah pretended to read the carton. "Yes. It says 'one hundred percent pulp.' "

"I hate pulp!" Herb declared.

5

"Me, too!" Bill agreed, making a face.

It wasn't the first time they'd had a breakfast discussion about pulp.

"Can't you buy orange juice without pulp?" Bill asked their mother.

"Can you strain it for us?" Herb asked Hannah.

"Can I have apple juice instead?" Bill asked.

"I don't want juice. I want milk," Herb decided.

Normally, this discussion would have made Hannah scream. But today, she reacted calmly. "One apple juice and one milk coming up," she said cheerfully.

"You certainly *are* in a good mood this morning," her mother commented.

Hannah handed Bill his apple juice, and he promptly spilled it.

After breakfast, Hannah helped her mother clean up the kitchen. "Nice day," Mrs. Fairchild said, peering out the window. "Not a cloud in the sky. It's supposed to go up to ninety."

Hannah laughed. Her mother was always giving weather reports. "Maybe I'll go for a long bike ride before it gets really hot," she told her mother.

She stepped out the back door and took a deep breath. The warm air smelled sweet and fresh. She watched two yellow-and-red butterflies fluttering side by side over the flower garden.

She took a few steps across the grass toward the garage. From somewhere down the block she could hear the low drone of a power mower.

Hannah gazed up at the clear blue sky. The sun felt warm on her face.

"Hey — *look out!*" an alarmed voice cried.

Hannah felt a sharp pain in her back.

She uttered a frightened gasp as she fell to the ground.

2

Hannah landed hard on her elbows and knees. She turned quickly to see what had hit her.

A boy on a bike. "Sorry!" he called. He jumped off the bike and let it fall to the grass. "I didn't see you."

I'm wearing Day-Glo green and orange, Hannah thought. Why couldn't he see me?

She climbed to her feet and rubbed the grass stains on her knees. "Ow," she muttered, frowning at him.

"I tried to stop," he said quietly.

Hannah saw that he had bright red hair, almost as orange as candy corn, brown eyes, and a face full of freckles.

"Why were you riding in my yard?" Hannah demanded.

"*Your* yard?" He narrowed his dark eyes at her. "Since when?"

"Since before I was born," Hannah replied sharply.

He pulled a leaf from her hair. "You live in that house?" he asked, pointing.

Hannah nodded. "Where do *you* live?" Hannah demanded. She examined her elbows. They were dirty, but not bruised.

"Next door," he said, turning toward the redwood ranch-style house across the driveway.

"Huh?" Hannah reacted with surprise. "You can't live there!"

"Why not?" he demanded.

"That house is empty," she told him, studying his face. "It's been empty ever since the Dodsons moved away."

"It's not empty now," he said. "I live there. With my mom."

How can that be? Hannah wondered. How could someone move in right next door without my knowing it?

I was playing with the twins back here yesterday, she thought, gazing hard at the boy. I'm sure that house was dark and empty.

"What's your name?" she asked.

"Danny. Danny Anderson."

She told him her name. "I guess we're neighbors," she said. "I'm twelve. How about you?"

"Me, too." He bent to examine his bike. Then he pulled out a tuft of grass that had gotten caught in the spokes of the back wheel. "How come I've never seen you before?" he asked suspiciously.

"How come I've never seen *you*?" she replied.

He shrugged. His eyes crinkled in the corners as a shy smile crossed his face.

"Well, did you just move in?" Hannah asked, trying to get to the bottom of the mystery.

"Huh-uh," he replied, concentrating on the bike.

"No? How long have you lived here?" Hannah asked.

"A while."

That's impossible! Hannah thought. There's no way he could have moved in next door without me knowing it!

But before she could react, she heard a high-pitched voice calling her from the house. "Hannah! Hannah! Herb won't give back my Gameboy!" Bill stood on the back stoop, leaning against the open screen door.

"Where's Mom?" Hannah shouted back. "She'll get it for you."

"Okay."

The screen door slammed hard as Bill went to find Mrs. Fairchild.

Hannah turned back to talk to Danny, but he had vanished into thin air.

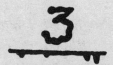

The mail usually came a little before noon. Hannah rushed eagerly down to the bottom of the drive and pulled open the mailbox lid.

No mail for her. No mail at all.

Disappointed, she hurried back to her room to write a scolding letter to her best friend, Janey Pace.

Dear Janey,

I hope you're having a good time at camp. But not too good — because you broke your promise. You said that you'd write to me every day, and so far, I haven't even received a crummy POST-CARD.

I am so BORED I don't know what to do! You can't imagine how little there is to do in Green-wood Falls when no one is around. It's really like DEATH!

I watch TV and I read a lot. Do you believe I've

already read ALL the books on our summer reading list? Dad promised to take us all camping in Miller Woods — BIG THRILL — but he's been working just about every weekend, so I don't think he will.

BORING!

Last night I was so bored, I marched the twins outside and built a little campfire behind the garage and pretended we were away at camp and told them a bunch of scary ghost stories.

The boys wouldn't admit it, of course, but I could see they enjoyed it. But you know how ghost stories freak me out. I started seeing weird shadows and things moving behind the trees. It was really kind of hilarious, I guess. I totally scared MYSELF.

Don't laugh, Janey. You don't like ghost stories, either.

My only other news is that a new boy moved into the Dodsons' old house next door. His name is Danny and he's our age, and he has red hair and freckles, and he's kind of cute, I think.

I've only seen him once. Maybe I'll have more to report about him later.

But now it's YOUR TURN to write. Come on, Janey. You promised. Have you met any cute guys at camp? Is THAT why you're too busy to write to me?

If I don't hear from you, I hope you get poison

ivy all over your body — especially in places where you can't scratch!

Love,
Hannah

Hannah folded the letter and stuffed it into an envelope. Her small desk stood in front of the bedroom window. Leaning over the desk, she could see the house next door.

I wonder if that's Danny's room? she thought, peering into the window just across the driveway. Curtains were pulled over the window, blocking her view.

Hannah pulled herself to her feet. She ran a hairbrush through her hair, then carried the letter to the front door.

She could hear her mother scolding the twins somewhere in the back of the house. The boys were giggling as Mrs. Fairchild yelled at them. Hannah heard a loud crash. Then more giggling.

"I'm going out!" she shouted, pushing open the screen door.

They probably didn't hear her, she realized.

It was a hot afternoon, no breeze at all, the air heavy and wet. Hannah's father had mowed the front lawn the day before. The freshly cut grass smelled sweet as Hannah made her way down the driveway.

She glanced over to Danny's house. No signs of

13

life there. The front door was closed. The big living room picture window appeared bare and dark.

Hannah decided to walk the three blocks to town and mail the letter at the post office. She sighed. Nothing else to do, she thought glumly. At least a walk to town will kill some time.

The sidewalk was covered with cut blades of grass, the green fading to brown. Humming to herself, Hannah passed Mrs. Quilty's redbrick house. Mrs. Quilty was bent over her garden, pulling up weeds.

"Hi, Mrs. Quilty. How are you?" Hannah called. Mrs. Quilty didn't look up.

What a snob! Hannah thought angrily. I know she heard me.

Hannah crossed the street. The sound of a piano floated from the house on the corner. Someone was practicing a piece of classical music, playing the same wrong note over and over, then starting the piece again.

I'm glad they're not *my* neighbors, Hannah thought, smiling.

She walked the rest of the way to town, humming to herself.

The two-story white post office stood across the tiny town square, its flag drooping on the pole in the windless sky. Around the square stood a bank, a barbershop, a small grocery, and a gas station. A few other stores, Harder's Ice-Cream Parlor, and a diner called Diner stretched behind the square.

Two women were walking out of the grocery. Through the barbershop window, Hannah could see Ernie, the barber, sitting in the chair, reading a magazine.

Real lively scene, she thought, shaking her head.

Hannah crossed the small, grassy square and dropped her letter in the mailbox in front of the post office door. She turned back toward home — but stopped when she heard the angry shouts.

The shouts were coming from behind the post office, Hannah realized. A man was screaming.

Hannah heard boys' voices. More yelling.

She began jogging around the side of the building, toward the angry voices.

She was nearly to the alley when she heard the shrill *yelp* of pain.

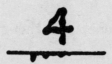

4

"Hey — !" Hannah called out and ran the rest of the way. "What's going on?"

A narrow alley stretched behind the post office. It was a hidden place where kids liked to hang out.

Hannah saw Mr. Chesney, the postmaster. He was shaking a fist angrily at a wiry brown mutt.

There were three boys in the alley. Hannah recognized Danny. He was hanging behind the two boys she didn't recognize.

The dog had its head lowered and was whimpering softly. A tall boy, thin and lanky with scraggly blond hair, grabbed the dog gently and bent down to comfort it.

"Don't throw stones at my dog!" the boy shouted at Mr. Chesney.

The other boy stepped forward. He was a short, stubby kid, kind of tough-looking, with spiky black hair. He glared at Mr. Chesney, his hands balled into fists at his sides.

Danny lingered away from the others, very pale, his eyes narrowed tensely.

"Get away! Go! I warned you!" Mr. Chesney snarled. He was a thin, red-faced man, entirely bald, with a bushy brown mustache under his pointed nose. He wore a tight-fitting gray wool suit, despite the summer heat.

"You don't have the right to hurt my dog!" the blond boy insisted, still cradling the mutt. The dog's stubby tail was wagging furiously now. The dog licked the boy's hand.

"This is government property," the postmaster replied sharply. "I'm warning you — get away from here. This isn't a hangout for you trouble-makers." He took a menacing step toward the three boys.

Hannah saw Danny take a few steps back, his expression frightened. The other two boys stood their ground, staring at the red-faced postmaster defiantly. They were big, Hannah saw. Bigger than Danny. They appeared to be older than Danny.

"I'm telling my dad you hurt Rusty," the blond boy said.

"Tell your dad you were trespassing," Mr. Chesney shot back. "And tell him you were rude and disrespectful. And tell him I'll file a complaint against all three of you punks if I catch you back here again."

"We're not punks!" the heavier boy shouted angrily.

Then all three boys turned and started running down the alley. The dog zigzagged excitedly at their heels, its stubby tail twitching wildly.

Mr. Chesney stormed past Hannah, muttering curses to himself. He was so angry, he pushed right past her as he made his way to the front of the post office.

What a jerk, Hannah thought, shaking her head. What is his problem, anyway?

All of the kids in Greenwood Falls hated Mr. Chesney. Mainly because he hated kids. He was always shouting at them to stop loitering in the square, or stop playing such loud music, or stop talking so loudly, or stop laughing so much, or to get out of his precious alley.

He acts as if he owns the whole town, Hannah thought.

At Halloween, Hannah and a bunch of friends had decided to go to Mr. Chesney's house and spray-paint his windows. But to their disappointment, Chesney was prepared for any Halloween trick-players. He stood at the ready in his front window, an enormous shotgun in his hand.

Hannah and her friends had gone on their way, disappointed and scared.

He knows how much we all hate him, Hannah realized.

And he doesn't care.

The alley was quiet now. Hannah headed back toward the town square, thinking about Danny. He had looked so frightened, so pale. So pale, he nearly seemed to fade away in the bright sunlight.

Danny's two friends didn't seem frightened at all, Hannah thought. They seemed angry and tough. Or maybe they were just acting tough because Mr. Chesney was being so horrible to the blond boy's dog.

Crossing the square, Hannah searched for signs of life. In his brightly lit shop, Ernie was still sitting in the barber chair, his face buried in a magazine. A blue station wagon had pulled into the gas station. A woman Hannah didn't recognize was hurrying to get to the bank before it closed.

No sign of Danny and his two friends.

I guess I'll go home and catch *General Hospital*, Hannah thought with a sigh. She crossed the street and made her way slowly toward home.

Tall trees, maples and birches and sassafras, lined the sidewalk. The leaves were so thick, they nearly blocked the sunlight.

It was cooler under their shade, Hannah realized as she walked under them.

She was halfway down the block when the dark figure slid out from behind a tree.

At first Hannah thought it was just the shadow cast by the wide trunk. But then, as her eyes adjusted to the shade, the figure became clear.

Hannah gasped and stopped walking.

She stared hard, squinting at him, struggling to bring him into focus.

He stood in a deep blue puddle of shadow. Dressed in black, he was tall and slender, his face completely hidden in darkness.

Hannah felt a cold shiver of fear roll down her body.

Who is he? she wondered. Why is he dressed like that?

Why is he standing so still, keeping in the shadows, staring back at me from the dark shade?

Is he trying to scare me?

He slowly raised a hand, motioning for her to come nearer.

Her heart fluttering in her chest, Hannah took a step back.

Is there really someone there?

A figure dressed in black?

Or am I seeing shadows cast by the trees?

She wasn't sure — until she heard the whisper:

"Hannah . . . Hannah . . ."

The whisper was as dry as the brush of tree leaves, and nearly as soft.

"Hannah . . . Hannah . . ."

A slender black shadow, motioning to her with

arms as bony as twigs, whispering to her. Such a dry, inhuman whisper.

"No!" Hannah cried.

She spun around and struggled to run. Her legs felt weak. Her knees didn't want to bend.

But she forced herself to run. Faster.

Faster.

Was he following her?

5

Panting loudly, Hannah crossed the street without stopping to look for traffic. Her sneakers pounded against the sidewalk as she ran.

One more block to go.

Is he following?

The shadows shifted and bent as she ran under the trees. Shadows on top of shadows, sliding over each other, gray on black, blue on gray.

"Hannah . . . Hannah . . ." The dry whisper.

Dry as death.

Calling to her from the shifting shadows.

He knows my name, she thought, gulping for breath, forcing her legs to keep moving.

And then she stopped.

And spun around.

"Who *are* you?" she shouted breathlessly. "What do you *want*?"

But he had vanished.

There was silence now. Except for Hannah's hard breathing.

22

Hannah stared into the tangle of late afternoon shadows. Her eyes darted over the shrubs and hedges of the yards on her block. She searched the spaces between the houses, the darkness behind an open garage door, the slanting gray square beside a small shed.

Gone. Vanished.

No sign of the black-enshrouded figure that had whispered her name.

"Whoa — !" she uttered out loud.

It was an optical illusion, she decided, her eyes still warily studying the front lawns.

No way.

She argued with herself. An optical illusion doesn't call your name.

There's nothing there, Hannah, she assured herself. Her breathing returned to normal. Nothing there.

You're making up more ghost stories. You're scaring yourself again.

You're bored and lonely, and so you're letting your imagination run away with you.

Feeling only a little better, Hannah jogged the rest of the way home.

Later, at dinner, she decided not to mention the shadow figure to her parents. They would never believe it anyway.

Instead, Hannah told them about the new family who had moved next door.

"Huh? Someone moved into the Dodsons' house?" Mr. Fairchild set down his fork and knife and stared across the table at Hannah from behind his square-framed horn-rimmed glasses.

"There's a boy my age," Hannah reported. "His name is Danny. He has bright orange hair and freckles."

"That's nice," Mrs. Fairchild replied distractedly, motioning for the twins to stop shoving each other and eat their dinners.

Hannah wasn't even sure her mother had heard her.

"How did they move in without us seeing them?" Hannah asked her father. "Did you see a moving truck or anything?"

"Huh-uh," Mr. Fairchild muttered, picking up his silverware and returning to his roast chicken.

"Well, don't you think it's *weird*?" Hannah demanded.

But before either parent could reply, Herb's chair toppled over backwards. His head hit the linoleum, and he began to howl.

Her mom and dad leapt off their chairs and bent to help him.

"I didn't push him!" Bill screamed shrilly. "Really. I didn't!"

Frustrated that her parents weren't interested in her big news, Hannah carried her plate to the kitchen. Then she wandered into her bedroom.

Making her way to her desk, she pushed aside the curtains and peered out the window.

Danny, are you in there? she wondered, staring at the curtains that covered his dark window. What are you doing right now?

The summer days seemed to float by. Hannah could barely remember how she passed the time. If only some of my friends were around, she thought wistfully.

If only *one* of my friends was around!

If only one of my friends would write.

Such a lonely summer . . .

She looked for Danny, but he never seemed to be around. When she finally saw him in his back yard one late afternoon, she hurried over to talk to him. "Hi!" she cried enthusiastically.

He was tossing a tennis ball against the back of the house and catching it. The ball made a loud *thock* each time it hit the redwood wall.

"Hi!" Hannah called again, jogging across the grass.

Danny turned, startled. "Oh. Hi. How's it going?" He turned back to the house and tossed the ball.

He was wearing a blue T-shirt over baggy black-and-yellow-striped shorts. Hannah stepped up beside him.

Thock. The ball hit the wall just below the gutter and bounced into Danny's hand.

"I haven't seen you around," Hannah said awkwardly.

"Uh-huh," was his brief reply.

Thock.

"I saw you behind the post office," she blurted out.

"Huh?" He spun the ball in his hand, but didn't throw it.

"A few days ago, I saw you in the alley. With those two guys. Mr. Chesney is a real jerk, isn't he?" Hannah said.

Danny snickered. "When he yells, his whole head turns bright red. Just like a tomato."

"A rotten tomato," Hannah added.

"What's his problem, anyway?" Danny asked, tossing the ball. *Thock.* "My friends and I — we weren't doing anything. Just hanging out."

"He thinks he's a big shot," Hannah replied. "He's always bragging how he's a *federal* employee."

"Yeah."

"What are you doing this summer?" she asked. "Just hanging around like me?"

"Kind of," he said. *Thock.* He missed the ball and had to chase it to the garage.

As he walked back toward the house, he gazed at her, as if seeing her for the first time. Hannah suddenly felt self-conscious. She was wearing a yellow top with grape jelly stains on the front, and her rattiest blue cotton shorts.

"Those two guys, Alan and Fred — they're the guys I usually hang out with," he told her. "Guys from school."

Thock.

How could he have friends from school? Hannah wondered. Didn't he just move here?

"Where do you go to school?" she asked, dodging out of the way as he backed up to catch the ball.

"Maple Avenue Middle School," he replied.

Thock.

"Hey — that's where I go!" Hannah exclaimed.

How come I've never seen him there? she wondered.

"Do you know Alan Miller?" Danny asked, turning to her, shading his eyes with one hand from the late afternoon sun.

Hannah shook her head. "No."

"Fred Drake?" he asked.

"No," she replied. "What grade are you in?"

"I'll be in eighth this year," he said, turning back to the wall.

Thock.

"Me, too!" Hannah declared. "Do you know Janey Pace?"

"No."

"How about Josh Goodman?" Hannah asked.

Danny shook his head. "Don't know him."

"Weird," Hannah said, thinking out loud.

Danny threw the tennis ball a little too hard, and it landed on the sloping gray-shingled roof. They both watched it hit, then roll down into the gutter. Danny sighed and, staring up at the gutter, made a disgusted face.

"How can we be in the same grade and not know any of the same kids?" Hannah demanded.

He turned to her, scratching his red hair with one hand. "I don't know."

"How weird!" Hannah repeated.

Danny stepped into the deep blue shadow of the house. Hannah squinted hard. He seemed to disappear in the wide rectangle of shadow.

That's impossible! she thought.

I would have seen him at school.

If we're in the same grade, there's no way I could have missed him.

Is he lying? Is he making this all up?

He had completely vanished in the shadow. Hannah squinted hard, waiting for her eyes to adjust.

Where is he? Hannah asked herself.

He keeps disappearing.

Like a ghost.

A ghost. The word popped in and out of her mind.

When Danny came back into view, he was pulling an aluminum ladder along the back wall of the house.

"What are you going to do?" Hannah asked, moving closer.

"Get my ball," he replied, and began climbing the ladder, his white Nikes hanging over the narrow metal rungs.

Hannah moved closer. "Don't go up there," she said, suddenly gripped with a cold feeling.

"Huh?" he called down. He was already halfway up the ladder, his head nearly level with the gutter.

"Come down, Danny." Hannah felt a wave of dread sweep over her. A heavy feeling in the pit of her stomach.

"I'm a good climber," he said, pulling himself up higher. "I climb everything. My mom says I should be in a circus or something."

Before Hannah could say anything more, he had clambered off the ladder and was standing on the sloping roof, his legs spread apart, his hands stretched high in the air. "See?"

Hannah couldn't shake the premonition, the heavy feeling of dread.

"Danny — please!"

Ignoring her shrill cry, he bent to pick the tennis ball from the gutter.

Hannah held her breath as he reached for the ball.

Suddenly, he lost his balance. His eyes went wide with surprise.

His sneakers slipped on the shingles. His hands shot up as if trying to grab onto something.

Hannah gasped, staring helplessly as Danny toppled headfirst off the roof.

6

Hannah screamed and shut her eyes.

I've got to get help, she thought.

Her heart pounding, she forced herself to open her eyes, and searched the ground for Danny. But to her surprise, he was standing in front of her, a mischievous grin on his face.

"Huh?" Hannah uttered a gasp of surprise. "You — you're okay?"

Danny nodded, still grinning.

He didn't make a sound, Hannah thought, staring hard at him. He landed without making a sound.

She grabbed his shoulder. "You're okay?"

"Yeah, I'm fine," Danny said calmly. "My middle name is Daredevil. Danny Daredevil Anderson. That's what my mom always says." He tossed the ball casually from hand to hand.

"You scared me to death!" Hannah cried. Her fright was turning to anger. "Why did you do that?"

He laughed.

"You could've been killed!" she told him.

"No way," he replied quietly.

She scowled at him, staring hard into his brown eyes. "Do you do stuff like that all the time? Falling off roofs just to scare people?"

His grin grew wider, but he didn't say anything. He turned away from her and tossed the tennis ball at the house.

Thock.

"You were falling headfirst," Hannah said. "How did you land on your feet?"

Danny chuckled. "Magic," he replied slyly.

"But — but — !"

"Hannah! Hannah!" She turned to see her mother calling to her from the back stoop.

"What is it?" Hannah shouted.

Thock.

"I have to go out for an hour. Can you come take care of Bill and Herb?"

Hannah turned back to Danny. "I've got to go. See you."

"See you," he replied, flashing her a freckle-faced grin.

Thock.

Hannah heard the sound of the ball against the redwood wall as she jogged across the driveway to her house. Again, she pictured Danny plummeting off the roof.

How did he do it? she wondered. How did he land on his feet so silently?

"I'll only be gone an hour," her mother said, searching her bag for the car keys. "How is it out? It's supposed to cloud up and rain tonight."

Another weather report, Hannah thought, rolling her eyes.

"Don't let them kill each other, if you can help it," Mrs. Fairchild said, finding the keys and shutting her bag.

"That was Danny," Hannah told her. "The new kid next door. Did you see him?"

"Huh-uh. Sorry." Mrs. Fairchild hurried to the door.

"You didn't see him?" Hannah called.

The screen door slammed.

Bill and Herb appeared and pulled Hannah into their room. "Chutes & Ladders!" Bill demanded.

"Yeah. Let's play Chutes & Ladders!" Herb echoed.

Hannah rolled her eyes. She *hated* that game. It was so lame. "Okay," she agreed with a sigh. She dropped down across from them on the rug.

"Yaaaay!" Bill cried happily, opening the gameboard. "You'll play?"

"Yeah. I'll play," Hannah told him unhappily.

"And can we cheat?" Bill asked.

"Yeah! Let's cheat!" Herb urged with grinning enthusiasm.

* * *

After dinner, the twins were upstairs, arguing with their parents over which of them got to take the *last* bath. They both hated baths and always fought to be the last.

Hannah helped clear the table, then wandered into the den. She was thinking about Danny as she made her way to the window.

Pushing aside the curtains, she pressed her forehead against the cool glass and stared across the drive to Danny's house.

The sun had lowered behind the trees. Danny's house was cast in heavy, dark shadows. The windows were covered with curtains and blinds.

Hannah realized she had never actually seen anyone inside the house. She had never seen Danny go into the house or come out of it.

She had never seen *anyone* come out of the house.

Hannah stepped back from the window, thinking hard. She remembered the morning she had met Danny, after he had run her down in the back yard. She had been talking to him — and he had *vanished* into thin air.

She thought about how he had seemed to disappear into the shadow at the side of his house, how she'd had to squint real hard to see him. And she thought about how he had seemed to float to the ground, landing silently from the roof.

Silent as a ghost.

"Hannah, what are you *thinking*?" she scolded herself.

Am I making up another ghost story?

She suddenly had so many questions running through her mind: How had Danny and his family moved in without her noticing? How could he be in her school, in her *grade*, without her ever seeing him there?

How come she didn't know his friends, and he didn't know hers?

It's all so *weird*, Hannah thought.

I'm not imagining it all. I'm *not* making it up.

What if Danny really is a ghost?

If only she had someone to talk to, someone to discuss Danny with. But her friends were all away. And her parents would certainly never listen to such a crazy idea.

I'll have to prove it myself, Hannah decided. I'll study him. I'll be scientific. I'll *observe* him. I'll *spy* on him.

Yes. I'll *spy* on him.

I'll go look in his kitchen window, she decided.

She stepped out onto the back stoop and pushed the screen door shut behind her. It was a warm, still night. A pale sliver of moon hung above the back yard in a royal-blue sky.

As Hannah headed across her back yard, taking long, rapid strides, crickets began to chirp loudly. Danny's house loomed in front of her, low and dark against the sky.

The ladder was still propped against the back wall.

Hannah crossed the driveway that separated her yard from his. Her heart pounding, she crept across the grass and climbed the three low concrete steps onto the back stoop. The kitchen door was closed.

She stepped up to the door, pressed her face close to the window, peered into the kitchen — and gasped.

7

Hannah gasped because Danny was staring back at her from the other side of the window.

"Oh!" she cried out and nearly toppled backwards off the narrow stoop.

Inside the house, Danny's eyes opened wide with surprise.

Behind him, Hannah could see a table set with bright yellow plates. A tall, slender, blonde-haired woman — Danny's mom, most likely — was pulling something out from a microwave oven onto the counter.

The door swung open. Danny poked his head out, his expression still surprised. "Hi, Hannah. What's up?"

"Nothing. I — uh — nothing, really," Hannah stammered. She could feel her cheeks grow hot, and knew she was blushing.

Danny's eyes burned into hers. His mouth turned up in a grin. "Well, do you want to come in or something?" he asked. "My mom is serving dinner, but — "

"No!" she cried, much too loudly. "I don't — I mean — I — "

I'm acting like a total jerk! she realized.

She swallowed hard, staring at his grinning face.

He's laughing at me!

"See you!" she cried, then leapt awkwardly off the stoop, nearly stumbling to the ground. Without looking back, she took off, running at full speed back to her house.

I've never been so embarrassed in my entire life! she thought miserably.

Never!

When she saw Danny come out of his house the next afternoon, Hannah hid behind the garage. Watching him walk his bike down the driveway, she felt her cheeks grow hot, felt embarrassed all over again.

If I'm going to be a spy, I'm going to have to be a lot cooler, she told herself. Last night, I lost it. I panicked.

It won't happen again.

She watched him climb on his bike and, standing up, pedal to the street. Pressed against the garage wall, she waited to see which direction he turned. Then she hurried into the garage to get her bike.

He's heading toward town, she saw. Probably

meeting those two boys. I'll let him get a head start, then I'll follow him.

She waited at the foot of the driveway, straddling her bike, watching Danny until he disappeared down the next block.

Sunlight filtered through the overhanging trees as she began pedaling, keeping a slow, steady pace as she rode after him. Mrs. Quilty was out weeding her garden as usual. This time, Hannah didn't bother to call hello.

A small white terrier chased her for half a block, yapping loudly with excitement, then finally giving up as Hannah pedaled away.

The school playground came into view. Several kids were playing softball on the corner diamond. Hannah looked for Danny, but he wasn't there.

She continued on into town. The sun felt warm on her face. She suddenly thought about Janey. Maybe I'll get a letter from her today, she thought.

She wished Janey were around to help spy on Danny. The two of them would be a great spy team, Hannah knew. She wouldn't have lost her cool like she had last night if Janey were around.

The town square came into view. The flag above the small, white post office was fluttering in a warm breeze. Several cars were parked in front of the grocery. Two women holding grocery bags were talking at the curb.

Hannah braked her bike and lowered her feet

to the ground. She shielded her eyes from the sun with one hand and searched for Danny.

Danny, where are you? she thought. Are you with your friends? Where did you go?

She pedaled across the small, grassy square toward the post office. Her bike bumped over the curb and she kept going, around the side of the building to the alley.

But the alley was silent and empty.

"Danny, where *are* you?" she called aloud in a quiet singsong. "Where *are* you?"

He was only a block ahead of me, she thought, scratching her short hair. Has he vanished into thin air again?

She rode back to the square, then checked out Harder's Ice-Cream Parlor and the diner.

No sign of him.

"Hannah, you're a *great* spy!" she laughed.

With a sigh of defeat, she turned around and headed for home.

She was nearly to her house when she saw the moving shadow.

It's back! she realized.

She shifted gears and started to pedal harder.

Out of the corner of her eye, she saw the shadow sliding across Mrs. Quilty's front lawn.

The dark figure floated silently over the grass toward her.

Hannah pedaled harder.

It's back. I didn't imagine it.

It's real.

But what can it be?

Standing up, she pedaled harder. Harder.

But the figure glided along with her, picking up speed, floating effortlessly.

She turned to see its arms stretch out toward her.

She gasped in terror.

Her legs suddenly felt as if they weighed a thousand pounds.

I — I can't move! she thought.

The shadow swept over her. She could feel the sudden cold.

Sticklike black arms reached out for her from the human-shaped shadow.

Its face — why can't I see its face? Hannah wondered, struggling to keep moving.

The shadow blocked the bright sun. The whole world was blackening beneath it.

Got to keep moving. Got to move, Hannah told herself.

The dark figure floated beside her, its arms outstretched.

Gaping in horror, Hannah saw bright red eyes glowing like embers from the blackness.

"Hannah . . ." it whispered. "Hannah . . ."

What does it want from me?

She struggled to keep pedaling, but her legs wouldn't cooperate.

"Hannah . . . Hannah . . ."

41

The dry whisper seemed to circle her, to wrap her in terror.

"Hannah . . ."

"No!" she screamed as she felt herself start to fall.

She struggled to keep her balance.

Too late.

She was falling. She couldn't stop herself.

"Hannah . . . Hannah . . ."

She reached out her hands to break her fall.

"Ooof!"

She gasped in pain as she landed hard on her side.

The bike fell on top of her.

The shadow figure, its red eyes glowing, moved in to capture her.

"Hannah! Hannah!"

"Hannah! Hannah!"

Its whisper became a shout.

"Hannah!"

Her side throbbed with pain. She struggled to catch her breath.

"What do you *want?*" she managed to cry. "Leave me alone! *Please!*"

"Hannah! It's me!"

She raised her head to see Danny standing above her. He straddled his bike, gripping the handlebars, staring down at her, his features tight with concern. "Hannah — are you okay?"

"The shadow — !" she cried, feeling dazed.

Danny lowered his bike to the grass and hurried over. He lifted her bike off her and set it down beside his. Then he reached for her hands. "Are you okay? Can you get up? I saw you fall. Did you hit a rock or something?"

"No." She shook her head, trying to clear it. "The shadow — he reached for me and — "

Danny's expression changed to bewilderment. "Huh? Who reached for you?" His eyes searched all around, then returned to her.

"He knew my name," Hannah said breathlessly. "He kept calling me. He followed me."

Danny studied her, frowning. "Did you hit your head? Do you feel dizzy, Hannah? Maybe I should go get some help."

"No . . . I . . . uh . . ." She gazed up at him. "Didn't you *see* him? He was dressed in black. He had these glowing red eyes — "

Danny shook his head, his eyes still studying her warily. "I only saw you," he said softly. "You were riding really fast. Over the grass. I saw you fall."

"You didn't see someone wearing black? A man? Chasing me?"

Danny shook his head. "There was no one else on the street, Hannah. Just me."

"Maybe I *did* bump my head," Hannah muttered, raising her hands to her short hair.

Danny reached out a hand. "Can you stand? Are you hurt?"

"I — I guess I can stand." She allowed him to pull her to her feet.

Her heart was still pounding. Her entire body felt shaky. Narrowing her eyes, she searched the front yards, her eyes lingering in the wide circles of shade from the neighborhood's old trees.

No one in sight.

"You really didn't see anyone?" she asked in a tiny voice.

He shook his head. "Just you. I was watching from over there." He pointed to the curb.

"But I thought . . ." Her voice trailed off. She could feel her face grow red.

This is embarrassing, she thought. He's going to think I'm a total nut case.

And then she thought, maybe I am!

"You were going so fast," he said, picking up her bike for her. "And there are so many shadows, from all the trees. And you were frightened. So maybe you imagined a guy dressed in black."

"Maybe," Hannah replied weakly.

But she didn't think so. . . .

High white clouds drifted over the sun the next afternoon as Hannah jogged down the driveway to the mailbox. Somewhere down the block, a dog barked.

She pulled down the lid and eagerly reached inside.

Her hand slid over bare metal.

No mail. Nothing.

Sighing with disappointment, she slammed the mailbox lid shut. Janey had promised to write every day. She had been gone for weeks, and Hannah still hadn't received even a postcard.

None of her friends had written to her.

As she trudged back up the driveway, Hannah

glanced at Danny's house. The white clouds were reflected in the glass of the big living room window.

Hannah wondered if Danny was home. She hadn't seen him since yesterday morning after falling off her bike.

My spying isn't going too well, she sighed.

Taking another glance at Danny's front window, Hannah headed back up the drive to the house.

I'll write to Janey again, she decided. I have to tell her about Danny and the frightening shadow figure and the weird things that have been happening.

She could hear the twins in the den, arguing loudly about which cartoon tape they wanted to see. Her mother was suggesting they go outside instead.

Hannah hurried to her room to get paper and a pen. The room felt hot and stuffy. She had tossed a pile of dirty clothes onto her desk. She decided to write her letter outside.

A short while later, she settled under the wide maple tree in the center of the front yard. A blanket of high clouds had rolled over the sky. The sun was trying to poke out from the white glare. The old, leafy tree protected her in comforting shade.

Hannah yawned. She hadn't slept well the night before. Maybe I'll take a nap later, she thought. But first, I have to write this letter.

Leaning back against the solid trunk, she began to write.

Dear Janey,

   How are you? I seriously hope you've fallen in the lake and drowned. That would be the only good excuse for not writing to me in all this time!

   How could you ABANDON me here like this? Next summer, one way or the other, I'm going to camp with you.

   Things are definitely WEIRD around here. Do you remember I told you about that boy who moved in next door? His name is Danny Anderson, and he's kind of cute. He has red hair and freckles and SERIOUS brown eyes.

   Well, don't laugh, Janey — but I think Danny is a GHOST!

   I can hear you laughing. But I don't care. By the time you get back to Greenwood Falls, I'm going to have PROOF.

   Please — don't tell the other girls in your bunk that your best friend has totally freaked until you read the rest of this. Here is my evidence so far:

   1. Danny and his family suddenly appeared in the house next door. I didn't see them move in, even though I've been home every day. Neither did my parents.

   2. Danny says he goes to Maple Avenue, and he says he's going into eighth grade just like us.

But how come we've never seen him? He hangs out with two guys I've never seen before. And he didn't know any of my friends.

3. Sometimes he vanishes — POOF — just like that. Don't laugh! And once he fell off the roof and landed on his feet — without making a SOUND! I'm SERIOUS, Janey.

4. Yesterday, I was being chased by a scary shadow, and I fell off my bike. And when I looked up, the shadow was gone, and Danny was standing in his place. And —

Uh-oh. This is starting to sound really crazy. I wish you were here so I could explain it better. It all sounds so DUMB in a letter. Like I'm really MESSED UP or something.

I know you're laughing at me. Well, go ahead.

Maybe I won't mail this letter. I mean, I don't want you to make jokes, or remind me of it for the rest of my life.

So, enough about me.

How's it going out there in the woods? I hope you were bitten by a snake and your entire body swelled up, and that's why I haven't heard from you.

Otherwise, I'm going to KILL you when you get back! Really!

WRITE!

Love,
Hannah

Yawning loudly, Hannah dropped her pen to the ground. She leaned back against the tree trunk and slowly read over the letter.

Is it too crazy to send? she wondered.

No. I *have* to send it. I *have* to tell somebody what's going on here. It's all too weird to keep to myself.

The sun had finally managed to burst through the clouds. The tree leaves above her head cast shifting shadows across the letter in her lap.

She glanced up into bright sunlight — and gasped, startled to see a face staring back at her.

"Danny — !"

"Hi, Hannah," he said quietly.

Hannah squinted up at him. His entire body was ringed by bright sunlight. He seemed to be shimmering in the light.

"I — I didn't see you," Hannah stammered. "I didn't know you were here. I — "

"Give me the letter, Hannah," Danny said softly but insistently. He reached out a hand for it.

"Huh? What did you say?"

"Give me the letter," Danny demanded, more firmly. "Give it to me now, Hannah."

She gripped the letter tightly and stared up at him. She had to shield her eyes. The bright sun seemed to shine right through him.

He hovered above her, his hand outstretched. "The letter. Hand it to me," he insisted.

"But — why?" Hannah asked in a tiny voice.

"I can't let you mail it," Danny told her.

"Why, Danny? It's *my* letter. Why can't I mail it to my friend?"

"Because you found out the truth about me," he said. "And there's no way I'll let you tell anyone."

9

"So, I'm right," Hannah said softly. "You're a ghost."

She shuddered, a wave of cold fear sweeping over her.

When did you die, Danny?

Why are you here? To haunt me?

What are you going to do to me?

Questions raced through her mind. Frightening questions.

"Give me the letter, Hannah," Danny insisted. "No one will ever read it. No one can know."

"But, Danny — " She stared up at him. Stared up at a ghost.

The golden sunlight poured through him. He shimmered in and out of view.

She raised a hand to shield her eyes.

He became too bright, too bright to look at.

"What are you going to do to me, Danny?" Hannah asked, shutting her eyes tight. "What are you going to do to me now?"

He didn't reply.

When Hannah opened her eyes, she stared up into *two* faces instead of one.

Two grinning faces.

Her twin brothers pointed at her and laughed. "You were asleep," Bill said.

"You were snoring," Herb told her.

"Huh?" Hannah blinked several times, trying to clear her mind. Her neck felt stiff. Her back ached.

"Here's how you were snoring," Herb said. He performed some hideous snuffling sounds.

Both boys fell to the grass, laughing. They rolled onto each other and began an impromptu wrestling match.

"I had a bad dream," Hannah said, more to herself than to her brothers. They weren't listening to her.

She climbed to her feet and stretched her arms above her head, trying to stretch away her stiff neck. "Ow." Falling asleep sitting up against a tree trunk was a bad idea.

Hannah gazed toward Danny's house. That dream was so real, she thought, feeling a cold chill down her back. So frightening.

"Thanks for waking me up," she told the twins. They didn't hear her. They were racing toward the back yard.

Hannah bent down and picked up the letter.

She folded it in half and made her way up the lawn to the front door.

Sometimes dreams tell the truth, she thought, her shoulders still aching. Sometimes dreams tell you things you couldn't know any other way.

I'm going to find out the truth about Danny, she vowed.

I'm going to find out the truth if it kills me.

The next evening, Hannah decided to see if Danny was home. Maybe he'd like to walk to Harder's and get ice-cream cones, she thought.

She told her mother where she was going and made her way across the back yard.

It had rained all day. The grass glistened wetly, and the ground beneath her sneakers was soft and marshy. A pale, crescent-shaped moon rose above wisps of black cloud. The night air felt tingly and wet.

Hannah crossed the driveway, then hesitated a few yards from Danny's back stoop. A square of dim yellow light escaped through the window on the back door.

She remembered standing at this door a few nights before and being totally embarrassed when Danny opened the door and she couldn't think of a thing to say.

At least this time I know what I'm going to say, she thought.

Taking a deep breath, Hannah stepped into the square of light on the stoop. She knocked on the window of the kitchen door.

She listened. The house was silent.

She knocked again.

Silence. No footsteps to answer the door.

She leaned forward and peered into the kitchen.

"Oh!" Hannah cried out in surprise.

Danny's mother sat at the yellow kitchen table, her back to Hannah, her hair glowing in the light of a low ceiling fixture. She had both hands wrapped around a steaming white coffee mug.

Why doesn't she answer the door? Hannah wondered.

She hesitated, then raised her fist and knocked loudly on the door. Several times.

Through the window, she could see that Danny's mother didn't react to the knocking at all. She lifted the white mug to her lips and took a long sip, her back to Hannah.

"Answer the door!" Hannah cried aloud.

She knocked again. And called: "Mrs. Anderson! Mrs. Anderson! It's me — Hannah! From next door!"

Under the cone of light, Danny's mother set the white mug down on the yellow table. She didn't turn around. She didn't move from her chair.

"Mrs. Anderson — !"

Hannah raised her hand to knock, then lowered it in defeat.

Why doesn't she hear me? Hannah wondered, staring at the woman's slender shoulders, at her hair gleaming down past the collar of her blouse.

Why won't she come to the door?

And then Hannah shivered with fear as she answered her own questions.

I know why she doesn't hear me, Hannah thought, backing away from the window.

I know why she doesn't answer the door.

Overcome with fear, Hannah uttered a low moan and backed away from the light, off the stoop, into the safety of the darkness.

10

Trembling all over, Hannah wrapped her arms around her chest, as if shielding herself from her frightening thoughts.

Mrs. Anderson doesn't hear me because she isn't real, Hannah realized.

She isn't real. She's a ghost.

Like Danny.

A ghost family has moved next door to me.

And here I am, standing in this dark back yard, trying to spy on a boy who isn't even alive! Here I am, trembling all over, cold with fear, trying to prove what I'm already sure of. He's a ghost. His mother is a ghost.

And I — I —

The kitchen light went out. The back of Danny's house was completely dark now.

The pale light from the crescent moon trickled onto the glistening, wet grass. Hannah stood, listening to the silence, trying to force away the frightening thoughts that crowded her mind until it felt as if her head were about to burst.

Where *is* Danny? she wondered.

Crossing the driveway, she headed back to her house. She could hear music and voices from the TV in the den. She could hear the twins' laughter floating out from the upstairs window of their room.

Ghosts, she thought, staring at the lighted windows, like bright eyes shining back at her.

Ghosts.

I don't *believe* in ghosts!

The thought made her feel a little less frightened. She suddenly realized her throat was dry. The night air felt hot and sticky against her skin.

She thought of ice cream again. Going to Harder's and getting a double-scoop cone seemed an excellent idea. Cookies-and-Cream, Hannah thought. She could already taste it.

She hurried into the house to tell her parents she was walking into town. At the doorway to the dark-paneled den, she stopped. Her parents, bathed in the glow of the TV screen, turned to her expectantly.

"What's up, Hannah?"

She had a sudden impulse to tell them everything. And so she did.

"The people next door, they're not alive," she blurted out. "They're ghosts. You know Danny, the boy my age? He's a ghost. I know he is! And his mother — "

"Hannah, please — we're trying to watch," her father said, pointing to the TV with the can of diet Coke in his hand.

They don't believe me, she thought.

And then she scolded herself: Of *course* they don't believe me. Who would believe such a crazy story?

In her room, she took a five-dollar bill from her wallet and shoved it into the pocket of her shorts. Then she brushed her hair, studying her face in the mirror.

I look okay, she thought. I don't *look* like a crazy person.

Her hair was damp from the wet night air. Maybe I'll let it grow, she thought, watching it fall into shape around her face. I should have *something* to show for this summer!

As she headed toward the front door, she heard loud bumping and banging above her head. The twins must be wrestling up in their room, she realized, shaking her head.

She stepped back out into the warm, wet darkness, jogged down the front lawn to the sidewalk, and headed toward town and Harder's Ice-Cream Parlor.

The tall, old-fashioned-looking streetlamps cast circles of blue-white light along the street. The trees, trembling in soft gusts of wind, rustled over the sidewalk as Hannah stepped beneath them.

Ghosts on the sidewalk, she thought with a shiver. They seemed to reach down for her with their leafy arms.

As she neared town, a strange feeling of dread swept over her. She quickened her pace as she passed the post office, its windows as black as the sky.

The town square was deserted, she saw. It wasn't even eight o'clock, and there were no cars passing through town, no one on the streets.

"What a hick town!" she muttered under her breath.

Behind the bank, she turned onto Elm Street. Harder's Ice-Cream Parlor stood on the next corner, a large red neon ice-cream cone in its window, casting a red glow onto the sidewalk.

At least Harder's stays open past dark, Hannah thought.

As she walked closer, she could see the glass front door of the small shop propped open invitingly.

She stopped a few feet from the door.

The feeling of dread suddenly became overpowering. Despite the heat of the night, she felt cold all over. Her knees trembled.

What's going on? she wondered. Why do I feel so strange?

As she stared through the red glare of the neon cone into the open doorway, a figure burst out.

Followed by another. And another.

Into the light, they ran, their faces twisted in fear.

Staring in surprise, she recognized Danny in front, followed by Alan and Fred.

They each held ice-cream cones in front of them.

They ran from the store, bent forward as if straining to flee as fast as possible. Their sneakers thudded against the pavement of the sidewalk.

Hannah heard loud, angry shouts from inside the shop.

Without realizing it, she had moved close to the door.

She could still hear the three boys running away. But she could no longer see them in the darkness.

She turned — and felt something hit her hard from behind.

"Ohh!" She cried out as she was thrown heavily onto the hard pavement.

11

Hannah landed hard on the sidewalk on her elbows and knees. The fall took her breath away.

A burning pain shot through her body.

What happened?

What hit me?

Gasping for breath, she raised her head in time to see Mr. Harder barrel past her. He was shouting at the top of his lungs for the boys to stop.

Hannah slowly pulled herself to her feet. *Whoa!* she thought. *Harder is really mad!*

Standing up straight, her bare knees throbbing with pain, her heart still thudding loudly, she glared after the store owner.

He could have at least said he was sorry he knocked me down, she thought angrily.

She leaned over to examine her knees in the light from the ice-cream parlor. Were they cut?

No. Just a little bruised.

Brushing off her shorts, she glanced up to see Mr. Harder hurrying back to the store. He was a short, fat man with curls of white hair around his round, pink face. He wore a long white apron that flapped in the wind as he walked, his fists swinging at his sides.

Hannah ducked back out of the light, behind a wide tree trunk.

A few seconds later, she could hear him back behind the counter, complaining loudly to his wife. "What is wrong with these kids?" he was bellowing. "They take ice cream and run without paying? Don't they have parents? Don't they have anyone to teach them right from wrong?"

Mrs. Harder murmured something to soothe her husband. Hannah couldn't hear the words.

With Mr. Harder's angry shouts filling the air, she crept out from behind the tree and hurried away, in the direction the boys had run.

Why did Danny and his friends pull such a stupid stunt? she wondered. What if they had been caught? Was it really worth being arrested, getting a police record just for an ice-cream cone?

Halfway down the block, she could still hear Mr. Harder bellowing with rage from inside his small shop. Hannah started to run, eager to get away from his angry voice. Her left knee ached.

The air suddenly felt stifling hot, heavy and damp. Strands of hair were matted against her forehead from sweat.

She pictured Danny running from the store, holding the ice-cream cone in one hand. She pictured the frightened expression on his face as he fled. She pictured Alan and Fred right behind him, their sneakers thudding against the pavement as they made their getaway.

And now she was running, too. She wasn't sure why.

Her left knee still ached from her fall. She was out of the town square now, running past dark houses and lawns.

She turned a corner, the streetlamp casting a cone of white light around her. More houses. A few porchlights lit. No one on the street.

Such a boring little town, she thought again.

She stopped short when she saw the three boys. They were halfway up the block, huddled behind a tall, wall-like hedge.

"Hey — you guys!" Her voice came out a whisper.

Running in the street, she made her way toward them quickly. As she came closer, she could see them laughing together, enjoying their ice-cream cones.

They hadn't seen her. Hannah made her way into the deep shadows on the other side of the street. Keeping in the dark, she crept closer, until she was in the yard across the street from them, hidden by a bushy evergreen shrub.

Fred and Alan were shoving each other playfully, enjoying their triumph over the store owner. Danny stood by himself, behind them against the tall hedge, silently licking his cone.

"Harder's was having a special tonight," Alan declared loudly. "Free ice cream!"

Fred hee-hawed and slapped Alan hard on the back.

Both boys turned to Danny. The light from the streetlamp made their faces look pale and green. "You looked real scared," Alan told Danny. "I thought you were going to puke your guts out."

"Hey, no way," Danny insisted. "I was the first one out of there, you know. You guys were so slow, I thought I'd have to come back and rescue you."

"Yeah. For sure," Fred replied sarcastically.

Danny's acting tough, Hannah realized. He's trying to be like them.

"That was kind of exciting," Danny said, tossing the remainder of his cone into the hedge. "But maybe we'd better be careful. You know. Not hang around there for a while."

"Hey, it's not like we robbed a bank or something," Alan said. "It was just ice cream."

Fred said something to Alan that Hannah couldn't hear, and the two boys started wrestling around, uttering high-pitched giggles.

"Hey, guys — not so loud," Danny warned. "I mean — "

"Let's go back to Harder's," Alan suggested. "I wanted *two* scoops!"

Fred hee-hawed and slapped Alan a high-five. Danny joined in the laughter.

"Hey, guys — we should get going," Danny said.

Before his friends could reply, the street filled with light.

Hannah turned to see two bright white lights looming toward them.

Car headlights.

The police, Hannah thought.

They're caught. All three of them are caught.

12

The car stopped.

Hannah peered out from behind the shrub.

"Hey, you kids — " the driver called to the boys in a gruff voice. He poked his head out the car window.

It isn't the police, Hannah realized, breathing a long sigh of relief.

The boys froze against the hedge. In the dim light from the streetlamp, Hannah could see that the driver was an elderly man, white-haired, wearing glasses.

"We're not doing anything. Just talking," Fred called to the man.

"Do any of you know how to get to Route 112?" the man asked. The light went on inside the car. Hannah could see a roadmap in the man's hand.

Fred and Alan laughed, relieved laughter. Danny continued to stare at the driver, his expression still frightened.

"Route 112?" the man repeated.

66

"Main Street turns into Route 112," Alan told the man, pointing in the direction the car was heading. "Go up two blocks. Then turn right."

The light went out in the car. The man thanked them and drove off.

The boys watched until the car had disappeared in the darkness. Fred and Alan slapped each other high-fives. Then Fred shoved Alan into the hedge. They all laughed giddily.

"Hey, look where we are," Alan said, surprised.

The boys turned toward the driveway. From her hiding place across the street, Hannah followed their gaze.

At the end of the hedge stood a tall wooden mailbox on a pole. A hand-carved swan's head perched on top of the box, which had graceful wings jutting out from its sides.

"It's Chesney's house," Alan said, making his way along the hedge toward the mailbox. He grabbed the wings with both hands. "Do you *believe* this mailbox?"

"Chesney carved it himself," Fred said, snickering. "What a dork."

"It's his pride and joy," Alan sneered. He pulled open the lid and peered inside. "Empty."

"Who would write to *him*?" Danny declared, trying to sound as tough as his two friends.

"Hey, I've got an idea, Danny," Fred said. He stepped behind Danny and started shoving him toward the mailbox.

"Whoa," Danny protested.

But Fred pushed him up to the mailbox. "Let's see how strong you are," Fred said.

"Hey, wait — " Danny cried.

Hannah leaned out from behind the low shrub. "Oh, wow," she muttered to herself. "*Now* what are they going to do?"

"Take the mailbox," she heard Alan order Danny. "I dare you."

"We dare you," Fred added. "Remember what you told us about dares, Danny? How you never turn one down?"

"Yeah. You told us you never turn down a dare," Alan said, grinning.

Danny hesitated. "Well, I — "

A heavy feeling of dread formed in the pit of Hannah's stomach. Watching Danny step toward Mr. Chesney's hand-carved mailbox, she suddenly had a premonition — a feeling that something really terrible was about to happen.

I've got to stop them, she decided.

Taking a deep breath, she stepped out from behind the bush.

As she started to call to them, everything went black.

"Hey — !" she cried aloud.

What had happened?

Her first thought was that the streetlamp had gone out.

But then Hannah saw the two red circles glowing in front of her.

The two glowing eyes surrounded by darkness.

The shadow figure rose up inches in front of her.

She tried to scream, but her voice was muffled in its heavy darkness.

She tried to run, but it blocked her path.

The red eyes burned into hers.

Closer. Closer.

It's got me now, Hannah knew.

13

"Hannah . . ." it whispered. "Hannah . . ."

So close, she could smell its hot, sour breath.

"Hannah . . . Hannah . . ." Its whisper like crackling, dead leaves.

The ruby eyes burned like fire. Hannah felt the darkness circle her, wrap around her tightly.

"Please — " was all she could manage to choke out.

"Hannah . . ."

And the light returned.

Hannah blinked, struggled to breathe.

The sour odor lingered in her nostrils. But the street was bright now.

Car headlights washed over her.

It — it's gone, Hannah realized. The lights had chased away the shadow figure.

But would it return?

As the car passed by, Hannah dropped to the ground behind the low evergreen shrub and struggled to catch her breath. When she looked up, the boys were still huddled in front of Mr. Chesney's hedge.

"Let's get going," Danny urged them.

"No way. Not yet," Alan said, stepping in front of Danny to block his way. "You're forgetting about our dare."

Fred shoved Danny toward the mailbox. "Go ahead. Take it."

"Hey, wait." Danny spun around. "I never said I'd do it."

"I dared you to take Chesney's mailbox," Fred told him. "Remember? You told us you never turned down a dare?"

Alan laughed. "Chesney will come out tomorrow and think his swan flew away."

"No, wait — " Danny protested. "Maybe it's a dumb idea."

"It's a *cool* idea. Chesney is a creep," Alan insisted. "Everyone in Greenwood Falls hates his guts."

"Take his mailbox, Danny," Fred challenged. "Pull it up. Come on. I dare you."

"No, I — " Danny tried to back away, but Fred held him from behind by the shoulders.

"You chicken?" Alan challenged.

"Look at the chicken," Fred said in a mocking, babyish voice. "Cluck cluck."

"I'm not a chicken," Danny snapped angrily.

"Prove it," Alan demanded. He grabbed Danny's hands and raised them to the carved wings that stretched from the sides of the mailbox. "Go ahead. Prove it."

"What a riot!" Fred declared. "The town postmaster — his mailbox flies away."

Don't do it, Danny, Hannah urged silently from her dark hiding place across the street. *Please — don't do it.*

Another set of car headlights made the three boys back away from the mailbox. The car rolled past without slowing.

"Let's go. It's getting late," Hannah heard Danny say.

But Fred and Alan insisted, teasing him, challenging him.

As Hannah stared into the white light of the streetlamp, Danny stepped up to Chesney's mailbox and grabbed the wings.

"Danny, wait — " Hannah cried.

He didn't seem to hear her.

With a loud groan, he began to tug.

It didn't budge.

He lowered his hands to the pole and wrapped them tightly around it just below the box.

He tugged again.

"It's in really deep," he told Alan and Fred. "I don't know if I can get it."

"Try again," Alan urged.

"We'll help you," Fred said, placing his hands above Danny's on the box.

"Let's all pull together," Alan urged. "At the count of three."

"*I wouldn't do that if I were you!*" exclaimed a gruff voice behind them.

They all turned to see Mr. Chesney glaring at them from the driveway, his face knotted in a furious snarl.

14

Mr. Chesney grabbed Danny's shoulders and pulled him away from the mailbox.

One of the wooden swan wings came off in Danny's hands. As Mr. Chesney wrestled him away, Danny let it drop to the ground.

"You punks!" Mr. Chesney sputtered, his eyes wide with rage. "You — you — "

"Let go of him!" Hannah screamed from across the street. But fear muffled her voice. Her cry came out a whisper.

With a loud groan, Danny pulled free of the man's grasp.

Without another word, the three boys were running, running down the middle of the dark street, their sneakers pounding loudly on the pavement.

"I'll remember you!" Mr. Chesney called after them. "I'll remember you. I'll see you again! And next time, I'll have my shotgun!"

Hannah watched Mr. Chesney bend to pick up the broken swan's wing. He examined the wooden wing, shaking his head angrily.

Then she began running, keeping in the dark front yards, hidden by hedges and low shrubs, running in the direction Danny and his friends had headed.

She saw the boys turn a corner, and kept running. Keeping well behind, she followed them through the town square, still deserted and dark. Even Harder's ice-cream parlor was closed now, the shop dark behind the red glare of the neon window sign.

Two dogs, tall, ungainly mutts with thin, shaggy frames, crossed the street in front of them, trotting slowly, out for their evening walk. The dogs didn't look up as the boys ran past.

Halfway up the next block, she saw Fred and Alan collapse beneath a dark tree, giggling up at the sky as they sprawled on the ground.

Danny leaned against the wide tree trunk, panting loudly.

Fred and Alan couldn't stop laughing. "Did you see the look on his face when that stupid wing dropped off?" Fred cried.

"I thought his eyes were going to pop out!" Alan exclaimed gleefully. "I thought his head was going to explode!"

Danny didn't join in their laughter. He rubbed

his right shoulder with one hand. "He really wrecked my shoulder when he grabbed me," he said, groaning.

"You should sue him!" Alan suggested.

He and Fred laughed uproariously, sitting up to slap each other high-fives.

"No. Really," Danny said quietly, still rubbing the shoulder. "He really hurt me. When he swung me around, I thought — "

"What a creep," Fred said, shaking his head.

"We'll have to pay him back," Alan added. "We'll have to — "

"Maybe we should stay away from there," Danny said, still breathing hard. "You heard what he said about getting his shotgun."

The other two boys laughed scornfully. "Yeah. For sure. He'd really come after us with a shotgun," Alan scoffed, brushing blades of freshly cut grass from his scraggly hair.

"The respected town postmaster, shooting at innocent kids," Fred said, snickering. "No way. He was just trying to scare us — right, Danny?"

Danny stopped rubbing his shoulder and frowned down at Alan and Fred, who were still sitting in the grass. "I don't know."

"Oooh, Danny is scared!" Fred cried.

"You're not scared of that old geek, are you?" Alan demanded. "Just because he grabbed your shoulder doesn't mean — "

"I don't know," Danny interrupted angrily.

"The old guy seemed pretty out of control to me. He was so angry! I mean, maybe he *would* shoot us to protect his precious mailbox."

"Bet we could make him a lot angrier," Alan said quietly, climbing to his feet, staring intently at Danny.

"Yeah. Bet we could," Fred agreed, grinning.

"Unless you're chicken, Danny," Alan said, moving close to Danny, challenge in his voice.

"I — it's getting late," Danny said, trying to read his watch in the dark. "I promised my mom I'd get home."

Fred climbed to his feet and moved next to Alan. "We should teach Chesney a lesson," he said, brushing blades of grass off the back of his jeans. His eyes gleamed mischievously in the dim light. "We should teach him not to pick on innocent kids."

"Yeah, you're right," Alan agreed, his eyes on Danny. "I mean, he hurt Danny. He had no business grabbing him like that."

"I've got to get home. See you guys tomorrow," Danny said, waving.

"Okay. See you," Fred called after them.

"At least we got some free ice cream tonight!" Alan exclaimed.

As Danny walked quickly away, Hannah could hear Alan and Fred giggling their gleeful, high-pitched giggles.

Free ice cream, she thought, frowning. Those

two guys are really looking for trouble.

She couldn't help herself. She had to say something to Danny. "Hey!" she called, running to catch up to him.

He spun around, startled. "Hannah — what are *you* doing here?"

"I — I followed you. From the ice-cream store," she confessed.

He snickered. "You saw everything?"

She nodded. "Why do you hang out with those two guys?" she demanded.

He scowled, avoiding her eyes, picking up his pace. "They're okay," he muttered.

"They're going to get in big trouble one of these days," Hannah predicted. "They really are."

Danny shrugged. "They just talk tough. They think it's cool. But they're really okay."

"But they stole ice-cream cones and — " Hannah decided she'd said enough.

They crossed the street in silence.

Hannah glanced up to see the pale crescent of moon disappear behind black wisps of cloud. The street grew darker. The trees shook their leaves, sending whispers all around.

Danny kicked a stone down the sidewalk. It clattered softly onto the grass.

Hannah suddenly remembered going over to Danny's house earlier to get him. In all the excitement of the stolen ice-cream cones and Mr. Chesney and his mailbox, she had completely forgotten what had happened on his back stoop.

"I — I went over to your house tonight," she started reluctantly. "Before I went into town."

Danny stopped and turned to her, his eyes studying hers. "Yeah?"

"I thought maybe you'd want to walk to town or something," Hannah continued. "Your mother was home. In the kitchen."

He continued to stare hard at her, as if trying to read her thoughts.

"I knocked and knocked on the kitchen door," Hannah said, tugging a strand of blonde hair off her forehead. "I could see your mother at the table. She had her back to me. She didn't turn around or anything."

Danny didn't reply. He lowered his eyes to the pavement and started walking again, hands shoved in his pockets.

"It was so strange," Hannah continued. "I knocked and knocked. Really loud. But it was like — like your mother was in a different world or something. She didn't answer the door. She didn't even turn around."

Their houses came into view ahead of them. A porchlight sent a yellow glow over Hannah's front lawn. On the other side of the driveway, Danny's house loomed in darkness.

Hannah's throat suddenly felt dry. She wished she could ask Danny what she really wanted to ask.

Are you a ghost? Is your mother a ghost, too?

That was the real question in Hannah's mind.

But it was too crazy. Too stupid.

How can you ask a person if he is real or not? If he is alive or not?

"Danny — why didn't your mother answer the door?" she asked quietly.

Danny turned at the bottom of her driveway, his expression set, his eyes narrowed. His face glowed eerily in the pale yellow light from the porch.

"Why?" Hannah repeated impatiently. "Why didn't she answer the door?"

He hesitated.

"I guess I should tell you the truth," he said finally, his voice a whisper, as soft as the whisper of the shuddering trees.

15

Danny leaned close to Hannah. She could see that his red hair was matted to his forehead by perspiration. His eyes burned into hers.

"There's a good reason why my mother didn't answer the door," Danny told her.

Because she's a ghost, Hannah thought. She felt a cold shiver roll down her back. A tremor of fear.

She swallowed hard. *Am I afraid of Danny?* she asked herself.

Yes. A little, she realized. Her scary dream about him flashed into her mind. *Yes. A little.*

"You see," Danny started, then hesitated. He cleared his throat. He shifted his weight nervously. "You see, my mom is deaf."

"Huh?" Hannah wasn't sure she had heard correctly. It wasn't at all what she was expecting.

"She got this inner-ear infection," Danny explained in a low voice, keeping his eyes trained on Hannah. "In both ears. A couple of years ago. The doctors treated it, but the infection spread.

They thought they could save one ear, but they couldn't. It made her completely deaf."

"You — you mean — ?" Hannah stammered.

"That's why she couldn't hear you knocking," Danny explained. "She can't hear anything at all." He lowered his eyes to the ground.

"I see," Hannah replied awkwardly. "I'm sorry, Danny. I didn't know. I thought . . . well, I didn't know *what* to think."

"Mom doesn't like people to know," Danny continued, backing toward his house. "She thinks people will feel sorry for her if they know. She hates to have people feeling sorry for her. She's a really good lip-reader. She usually fools people."

"Well, I won't say anything," Hannah replied. "I mean, I won't tell anyone. I — " She suddenly felt very stupid.

Her head lowered, she made her way up the driveway toward her front walk.

"See you tomorrow," Danny called.

"Yeah. Okay," she replied, thinking about what he had just told her.

She looked up to wave good-night to him.

But he had vanished.

Hannah turned and began jogging around the side of the house toward the back door. Danny's words troubled her. She realized all of her thoughts about ghosts may have been a big mistake.

Her parents were always predicting that some day her imagination would run away with her.

Now maybe it has, Hannah thought unhappily. Maybe I've totally lost it.

She turned the corner of the house and started toward the back door, her sneakers squishing on the soft, wet ground.

The light over the porch sent a narrow cone of white light onto the concrete stoop.

Hannah was nearly to the door when the dark figure, wrapped in black shadow, its red eyes glowing like hot coals, stepped into the light, blocking her path.

"Hannah — stay away!" It whispered, pointing menacingly at her with one long, shadowy finger.

16

Gripped with horror, Hannah thought she saw the shadow of an evil grin inside the deeper shadow that hovered over the stoop. "Hannah, stay away. Stay away from DANNY!"

"*Nooooooooooo!*"

In her panic, Hannah didn't even realize that the howl came from her own throat.

The red eyes glowed brighter in reaction to her scream. The fiery stare burned into her eyes, forcing her to shield her face with both hands.

"Hannah — listen to my warning." The dreadful dry whisper.

The whisper of death.

The sinewy black finger, outlined in the white porchlight, pointed to her, threatened her again.

And again Hannah cried out in a voice hoarse with terror: "*Nooooooo!*"

The dark figure swept closer.

Closer.

And then the kitchen door swung open, throwing a long rectangle of light over the yard.

"Hannah — is that you? What's going on?"

Her father stepped into the light, his features knotted with concern, his eyes peering into the darkness through his square eyeglasses.

"Dad — !" Hannah's voice caught in her throat. "Look out, Dad — he — he — " Hannah pointed.

Pointed to empty air.

Pointed to the empty rectangle of light from the kitchen door.

Pointed to nothing.

The shadow figure had disappeared once again.

Her mind spinning in confusion, feeling dazed and terrified, she hurried past her father, into the house.

She had told her parents about the frightening dark figure with the glowing red eyes. Her father carefully searched the back yard, his flashlight playing over the lawn. He found no footprints in the soft, wet ground, no sign at all of an intruder.

Hannah's mother had gazed intently at her, studying her, as if trying to find some kind of answer in Hannah's eyes.

"I — I'm not crazy," Hannah stammered angrily.

Mrs. Fairchild's cheeks turned pink. "I know that," she replied tensely.

"Should I call the police? There's nothing back there," Mr. Fairchild said, scratching his thinning brown hair, his eyeglasses reflecting the light from the kitchen ceiling.

"I'll just go to bed," Hannah told them, moving abruptly to the door. "I'm really tired."

Her legs felt trembly and weak as she hurried down the hall to her room.

Sighing wearily, she pushed open her bedroom door.

The dark shadow figure was waiting for her by her bed.

17

Hannah gasped and started to back away.

But as the hall light fell into the bedroom, she realized she wasn't staring at the frightening figure after all.

She was staring at a longsleeved, dark sweater she had tossed over the bedpost at the foot of her bed.

Hannah gripped the sides of the doorway. She couldn't decide whether to laugh or cry.

"What a night!" she exclaimed out loud.

She clicked on the bedroom ceiling light, then closed the door behind her. As she made her way over to the bed to pull the sweater off the bedpost, she was shaking all over.

She pulled off her clothes quickly, tossing them onto the floor, and put on a nightshirt. Then she climbed under the covers, eager to get to sleep.

But she couldn't stop her mind from whirring over all that had happened. She couldn't stop the frightening pictures from playing in her head, over and over.

The shadows of tree limbs from the front yard shifted and bobbed across the ceiling. Normally, she found their silent dance soothing. But tonight the moving shadows frightened her, reminded her of the menacing dark figure that had called her name.

She tried to think about Danny instead. But those thoughts were just as troubling.

Danny is a ghost. Danny is a ghost.

The phrase repeated again and again in her mind.

He *had* to be lying about his mother, Hannah decided. He made up the story about her being deaf because he doesn't want me to figure out that *she's* a ghost, too.

Questions, questions.

Questions she couldn't answer.

If Danny is a ghost, what is he doing here? Why did he move in next door to me?

Why does he hang out with Alan and Fred? Are they ghosts, too?

Is that why I've never seen them at school or in town before? Is that why I've never seen any of them? They're all ghosts?

Hannah shut her eyes, trying to force all the questions from her mind. But she couldn't stop thinking about Danny — and the dark shadow figure.

Why did the dark figure tell me to stay away from Danny? Is it trying to keep me from proving that Danny is a ghost?

Finally, Hannah fell asleep. But even in sleep, her troubled thoughts pursued her.

The sinewy black shadow followed her into her dreams. In the dream, she was standing in a gray cave. A fire burned brightly, far in the distance at the mouth of the cave.

The black figure, its red eyes glowing brighter than the fire, moved toward Hannah. Closer. And closer.

And when the black figure came so close, close enough for Hannah to reach out and touch it, the shadow figure reached up with its sticklike arms and pulled itself apart.

It reached up with its ebony hands and with bonelike fingers, pulled away the darkness where its face should be — revealing Danny underneath.

Danny, leering at her with glowing red eyes that burned into hers — until she woke up gasping for breath.

No, she thought, staring out the window at the gray dawn. *No. Danny isn't the black shadow.*

No way.

It isn't Danny.

It can't be Danny. The dream makes no sense.

Hannah sat up. Her bedclothes were damp from perspiration. The air in the room hung heavy and sour.

She kicked off the covers and lowered her feet to the floor.

She knew only one thing for certain after her long night of frightening thoughts.

She had to talk to Danny.

She couldn't spend another night like this.

She had to find out the truth.

The next morning, after breakfast, she saw him kicking a soccer ball around in his back yard. She pulled open the kitchen door and ran outside. The screen door slammed loudly behind her as she began to run to him.

"Hey, Danny — " she called. "Are you a ghost?"

18

"Huh?" Danny glanced at her, then kicked the black-and-white soccer ball against the side of the garage. He was wearing a navy-blue T-shirt over denim shorts. He had a blue-and-red Cubs cap pulled down over his red hair.

Hannah ran full speed across the driveway and stopped a few feet from him. "Are you a ghost?" she repeated breathlessly.

He wrinkled his forehead, squinting at her. The ball bounced across the grass. He stepped forward and kicked it. "Yeah. Sure," he said.

"No. Really," Hannah insisted, her heart pounding.

The ball bounced high off the garage, and he caught it against his chest. "What did you say?" He scratched the back of a knee.

He's staring at me as if I'm nuts, Hannah realized.

Maybe I am.

"Never mind," she said, swallowing hard. "Can I play?"

"Yeah." He dropped the ball to the grass. "How ya doing?" he asked. "You okay today?"

Hannah nodded. "Yeah. I guess."

"That was pretty wild last night," Danny said, kicking the ball gently to her. "I mean, at Mr. Chesney's."

The ball got by Hannah. She chased after it and kicked it back. Normally, she was a good athlete. But this morning she was wearing sandals, not the best for kicking a soccer ball.

"I really got scared," Hannah admitted. "I thought that car that stopped was the police and — "

"Yeah. It was kind of scary," Danny said. He picked the ball up and hit it back to her with his head.

"Do Alan and Fred really go to Maple Avenue School?" Hannah asked. The ball hit her ankle and rolled toward the driveway.

"Yeah. They're going to be in ninth grade," Danny told her, waiting for her to kick the ball back.

"They're not new kids? How come I've never seen them?" She kicked the ball hard.

Danny moved to his right to get behind it. He snickered. "How come they've never seen *you*?"

He isn't giving me any straight answers, Hannah realized. *I think my questions are making him nervous. He knows I'm starting to suspect the truth about him.*

"Alan and Fred want to go back to Chesney's," Danny told her.

"Huh? They what?" She missed the ball and kicked up a clod of grass. "Ow. I can't play soccer in sandals!"

"They want to go back tonight. You know. To pay Chesney back for scaring us. He really hurt my shoulder."

"I think Alan and Fred are really looking for trouble," Hannah warned.

Danny shrugged. "Nothing *else* to do in this town," he muttered.

The ball rolled between them.

"I've got it!" they both yelled in unison.

They both chased after the ball. Danny got to it first. He tried to kick it away from her. But his foot landed on top of the ball. He stumbled over it and went sprawling onto the grass.

Hannah laughed and jumped over him to get to the ball. She kicked it against the side of the garage, then turned back to him, smiling triumphantly. "One for me!" she declared.

He sat up slowly, grass stains smearing the chest of his T-shirt. "Help me up." He reached up his hands to hers.

Hannah reached to pull Danny up — and her hands went right through him!

19

They both uttered startled cries.

"Hey, come on! Help me up," Danny said.

Her heart pounding, Hannah tried to grab his hands again.

But again her hands went right through his.

"Hey — !" Danny cried, his eyes wide with alarm. He jumped to his feet, staring at her hard.

"I knew it," Hannah said softly, raising her hands to her cheeks. She took a step back, away from him.

"Knew it? Knew *what*?" He continued to stare at her, his face filled with confusion. "What's going on, Hannah?"

"Stop pretending," Hannah told him, suddenly feeling cold all over despite the bright morning sunshine. "I know the truth, Danny. You're a ghost."

"Huh?" His mouth dropped open in disbelief. He pulled off his Cubs cap and scratched his hair, staring hard at her all the while.

"You're a ghost," she repeated, her voice trembling.

"Me?" he cried. "No way! Are you *crazy*? I'm not a ghost!"

Without warning, he stepped in front of her and shot his hand out at her chest.

Hannah gasped as his hand went right through her body.

She didn't feel a thing. It was as if she weren't there.

Danny cried out and jerked his hand back as if he had burned it. He swallowed hard, his expression tight with horror. "Y-you — " he stammered.

Hannah tried to reply, but the words caught in her throat.

Giving her one last horrified glance, Danny turned and began running at full speed toward his house.

Hannah stared helplessly after him until he disappeared through the back door. The door slammed hard behind him.

Dazed, Hannah turned and began to run home.

She felt dizzy. The ground seemed to spin beneath her. The blue sky shimmered and became blindingly bright. Her house tilted and swayed.

"Danny's not the ghost," Hannah said out loud. "I finally know the truth. Danny's not the ghost. *I am*!"

20

Hannah stepped up to the back door, then hesitated.

I can't go back in now, she thought. I have to think.

Maybe I'll take a walk or something.

She closed her eyes, trying to force her dizziness away. When she opened them, everything seemed brighter, too bright to bear.

Stepping carefully off the back stoop, she headed toward the front, her head spinning.

I'm a ghost.

I'm not a real person anymore.

I'm a ghost.

Voices broke into Hannah's confused thoughts. Someone was approaching.

She ducked out of sight behind the big maple tree and listened.

"It's a perfectly lovely house." Hannah recognized Mrs. Quilty's voice.

"My cousin from Detroit looked at it last week,"

another woman said. Hannah didn't recognize her. Peering out from behind the tree trunk, Hannah saw that it was a thin, haggard-looking woman wearing a yellow sundress. She and Mrs. Quilty were standing halfway up the drive, admiring Hannah's house.

Afraid she might be seen, Hannah ducked back behind the tree.

"Did your cousin like the house?" Mrs. Quilty asked her companion.

"Too small," was the curt reply.

"What a shame," Mrs. Quilty said with a loud sigh. "I just hate having an empty house on the block."

But it's not empty! Hannah thought angrily. I live here! My whole family lives here — don't we?

"How long has it been vacant?" the other woman asked.

"Ever since it was rebuilt," Hannah heard Mrs. Quilty reply. "You know. After that dreadful fire. I guess it was five years ago."

"Fire?" Mrs. Quilty's friend asked. "That was before I moved here. Did the whole house burn down?"

"Pretty much," Mrs. Quilty told her. "It was so dreadful, Beth. Such a tragedy. The family trapped inside. Such a beautiful family. A young girl. Two little boys. They all died that night."

My dream! Hannah thought, gripping the tree trunk to hold herself up. *It wasn't a dream. It was a real fire. I really died that night.*

Tears streamed down Hannah's face. Her legs felt weak and trembly. She leaned against the rough bark of the tree and listened.

"How did it happen?" Beth, Mrs. Quilty's friend, asked. "Do they know what started the fire?"

"Yes. The kids had some kind of campfire out back. Behind the garage," Mrs. Quilty continued. "When they went inside, they didn't put it out completely. The house caught fire after they'd gone to sleep. It spread so quickly."

Hannah saw the two women peering thoughtfully at the house from their position on the driveway. They were shaking their heads.

"The house was gutted, then completely rebuilt," Mrs. Quilty was saying. "But no one ever moved in. It's been five years. Can you imagine?"

I've been dead for five years, Hannah thought, letting the tears roll down her cheeks. No wonder I didn't know Danny or his friends.

No wonder I haven't gotten any letters from Janey. No wonder I haven't heard from any of my friends.

I've been dead for five years.

Now, Hannah understood why sometimes time seemed to stand still, and sometimes it floated by so quickly.

Ghosts come and go, she thought sadly. Sometimes I'm solid enough to ride a bike or kick a soccer ball. And sometimes I'm so flimsy, someone's hand goes right through me.

Hannah watched the two women make their way down the block until they disappeared from view. Clinging to the tree trunk, she made no attempt to move.

It was all beginning to make sense to Hannah. The dreamlike summer days. The loneliness. The feeling that something wasn't right.

But what about Mom and Dad? she asked herself, pushing herself away from the tree. What about the twins? Do they *know*? Do they know that we're all ghosts?

"Mom!" she shouted, running to the front door. "Mom!"

She burst into the house and ran through the hall to the kitchen. "Mom! Mom! Where *are* you? Bill? Herb?"

Silence.

No one there.

They were all gone.

21

"Where *are* you?" Hannah cried aloud. "Mom! Bill! Herb!"

Were they gone *forever*?

We're *all* ghosts, she thought miserably. *All*.

And now they've left me here by myself.

Her heart pounding, she gazed around the kitchen.

It was bare. Empty.

No cereal boxes on the counter where they were usually kept. No funny magnets on the refrigerator. No curtains on the window. No clock on the wall. No kitchen table.

"Where *are* you?" Hannah called desperately.

She pushed away from the counter and went running through the house.

All empty. All bare.

No clothing. No furniture. No lamps or posters on the wall or books in the bookshelves.

Gone. Everything gone.

They've left me here. A ghost. A ghost all by myself.

"I've *got* to talk to someone," she said aloud. "Anyone!"

She searched desperately for a telephone until she found a red one on the bare kitchen wall.

Who can I call? Who?

No one.

I'm dead.

I've been dead for five years.

She picked up the receiver and brought it to her ear.

Silence. The phone was dead, too.

With a hopeless cry, Hannah let the receiver fall to the floor. Her heart thudding, tears once again rolling down her cheeks, she flung herself down onto the bare floor.

Sobbing softly to herself, she buried her head in her arms and let the darkness sweep over her.

When she opened her eyes, the darkness remained.

She pulled herself up, not sure at first where she was. Feeling shaky and tense, she raised her eyes to the kitchen window. Outside, the sky was blue-black.

Night.

Time floats in and out when you're a ghost, Hannah realized. That's why the summer has seemed so short and so endless at the same time. She stretched her arms toward the ceiling, then wandered from the kitchen.

"Anyone home?" she called.

She wasn't surprised by the silence that greeted her question.

Her family was gone.

But where?

As she made her way through the dark, empty hallway toward the front of the house, she had another premonition. Another feeling of dread.

Something bad was going to happen.

Now? Tonight?

She stopped at the open front door and peered through the screen door. "Hey — !" Danny was on his bike, pedaling slowly down his driveway.

Impulsively, Hannah pushed open the screen door and ran outside. "Hey — Danny!"

He slowed his bike and turned to her.

"Danny — wait!" she called, running across her yard toward him.

"No — please!" His face filled with fright. He raised both hands as if to shield himself.

"Danny — ?"

"*Go away!*" he screamed, his voice shrill from terror. "*Please — stay away!*" He gripped the handlebars and began pedaling furiously away.

Hannah jumped back, stunned and hurt. "Don't be afraid of me!" she shouted after him, cupping her hands around her mouth to be heard. "Danny, please — don't be afraid!"

Leaning over the handlebars, he rode away without looking back.

Hannah uttered a hurt cry.

As Danny disappeared down the block, the feeling of dread swept over her.

I know where he's going, she thought.

He's meeting Alan and Fred, and they're going to Mr. Chesney's house. They're going to get their revenge on Mr. Chesney.

And something very bad is going to happen.

I'm going there, too, Hannah decided.

I *have* to go, too.

She hurried to the garage to get her bike.

Mr. Chesney had repaired his mailbox, Hannah saw. The hand-carved swan wings floated out from the pole, which had been returned to its erect position.

Crouching behind the same low evergreen, Hannah watched the three boys across the street. They hesitated at the edge of Mr. Chesney's yard, hidden from the house by the tall hedge.

In the pale white light of the streetlamp, Hannah could see them grinning and joking. Then she saw Fred shove Danny toward the mailbox.

Hannah raised her gaze beyond the hedge to Mr. Chesney's small house. Orange light glowed dimly from the living room window. The porchlight was on. The rest of the house sat in darkness.

Was Mr. Chesney home? Hannah couldn't tell.

His beat-up old Plymouth wasn't in the driveway.

Hannah crouched behind the evergreen. Its prickly branches bobbed in a light breeze.

She watched Danny struggle to pull up the mailbox. Alan and Fred were standing behind him, urging him on.

Danny gripped both jutting wings and pulled.

Fred slapped him on the back. "Harder!" he cried.

"What a wimp!" Alan declared, laughing.

Hannah kept glancing nervously up to the house. The boys were so noisy. What made them so sure that Mr. Chesney wasn't home?

What made them so sure that Chesney wouldn't keep his promise and come after them with his shotgun?

Hannah shuddered. She felt a trickle of perspiration slide down her forehead.

She watched Danny tug furiously at the mailbox. With a hard pull, he tilted it at an angle.

Fred and Alan cheered gleefully.

Danny began to rock the mailbox, pushing it with his shoulder, then pulling it back. It was coming loose, tilting farther with each push, each pull.

Hannah heard Danny's loud groan as he gave it a final strong push — and the mailbox fell onto its side on the ground. He backed away, a triumphant smile on his face.

Fred and Alan cheered again and slapped him high-fives.

Fred picked up the mailbox, hoisted it on his shoulder, and paraded back and forth in front of the hedge with it, as if it were an enemy flag.

As they celebrated their triumph, Hannah again glanced over the hedge to the dimly lit house.

No sign of Mr. Chesney.

Maybe he wasn't home. Maybe the boys would get away without getting caught.

But why did Hannah still have the heavy feeling of dread weighing her down, chilling her body?

She gasped as she saw a shadow slide past the corner of the house.

Mr. Chesney?

No.

Squinting hard into the dim light, Hannah felt her heart begin to thud against her chest.

No one there. But what was that shadow?

She had definitely seen it, a shape darker than the long night shadows, slithering against the grayness of the house.

The boys' loud voices interrupted her thoughts, drawing her attention away from the house.

Fred had tossed the mailbox into the hedge. Now they had moved toward the driveway. They were discussing something, arguing loudly. Alan laughed. Fred gave Alan a playful shove. Danny was saying something, but Hannah couldn't hear his words.

Get away, Hannah urged them in her mind. *Get*

away from there. You pulled your stupid prank, had your stupid revenge.

Now get away — before you get caught.

The evergreen limbs bobbed silently in a gust of hot wind. Hannah stepped back into the darkness, her eyes on the boys.

They were huddled together at the bottom of the driveway. They were talking excitedly, all three at once. Then Hannah saw a flicker of light. It glowed for a moment, then went out.

It was a match, Hannah realized.

Alan was holding a large box of kitchen matches.

Hannah glanced nervously at the house. All was still. No Mr. Chesney. No shadows slithering across the wall.

Go home. Please, go home, she silently urged the boys.

But to her dismay, they turned and began jogging up the gravel driveway. They ducked low as they ran, trying not to be seen from the house.

What are they doing? Hannah wondered, feeling all of her muscles tighten in dread. A shiver of fear ran down her back as she stepped out from behind the evergreen.

What are they going to do?

She made her way quickly across the street and ducked in front of the hedge, her heart pounding.

She couldn't hear them. They must be nearly up to the house by now.

Should she follow them?

She stood up slowly and raised herself on tiptoes to see over the hedge.

The three boys, Alan in the lead, followed by Danny and Fred, were bent low, running rapidly across the front of the house. Caught in the dim orange glow of light from the window, Hannah could see their determined expressions.

Where are they going? What are they planning?

Hannah watched them run into the darkness around the side of the house.

Still no sign of Mr. Chesney.

Keeping close to the hedge, Hannah made her way to the driveway. Then, without thinking about it, without even realizing it, she was running, too.

She stopped short as she saw Alan shoving Danny up into an open window. Then Fred stepped forward, lifted his hands to the window ledge, and allowed Alan to give him a boost.

No — please! Hannah wanted to cry.

Don't go into the house! Don't go in there!

But she was too late.

All three of them had climbed into the house.

Breathing hard, Hannah began to creep toward the window.

But halfway there, she felt something grab her leg and hold her in place.

22

Hannah uttered a silent cry.

She struggled to free her leg — and quickly realized she had stepped into a coiled garden hose.

Exhaling loudly, she lifted her foot out of it and crept the rest of the way to the open window.

This side of the house was covered in darkness. The window was too high for Hannah to see into the room.

Standing beneath the window, Hannah could hear the boys' sneakers thudding on bare floorboards. She could hear whispering voices and high-pitched, muffled laughter.

What are they doing in there? she wondered, her entire body tight with fear.

Don't they realize how much trouble they could get into?

Bright lights against the side of the house made Hannah jump back with a startled cry.

She dropped to the ground and spun around. And saw headlights through the tall hedge. Car headlights floating toward the driveway.

Mr. Chesney?

Was he returning home? Returning home in time to catch the three intruders in his house?

Hannah opened her mouth to call out a warning to the boys. But her voice caught in her throat.

The headlights floated past. The darkness rolled back over the yard.

The car rumbled silently on.

It wasn't Mr. Chesney, Hannah realized.

She struggled to her feet and returned to her place below the window. She decided she had to let the boys know she was there. She had to get them *out* of there!

"Danny!" she called, wrapping her hands around her mouth as a megaphone. "Get out! Come on — get out *now!*"

The feeling of dread weighed her down. She shouted up to the window again. "Come out. Hurry — please!"

She could hear their muffled voices inside. And she could hear the scrape of sneakers on the floor.

Staring up at the window, she saw a light come on. Orange light, dim at first, then brighter.

"Are you *crazy*?" she shouted in to them. "Turn off the lights!"

Why on earth were they turning on lights?

Did they *want* to get caught?

"Turn off the lights!" she repeated in a high, shrill, frightened voice.

But the orange light grew brighter, became a bright yellow.

And as she stared in horror, Hannah realized the light was flickering.

Not lamp light.

Fire light.

Fire!

They had set a fire!

"No!" she screamed, raising her hands to the sides of her face. "No! Get out! Get out of there!"

She could smell smoke now. She could see the reflection of the leaping flames in the window glass.

She started to shout to them again — but stopped when she saw the shadow move toward her on the wall of the house.

Hannah stopped and turned her stare.

And saw the dark figure, blacker than the night, its red eyes glowing brightly from the blackness of its face.

It stepped silently toward her, floating rapidly over the tall, weed-strewn grass. Its red eyes appeared to light up as it neared.

"Hannah — stay away!" the moving shadow called in a voice as dry as dead leaves.

"Hannah — stay away."

"Nooooo!" Hannah uttered a frightened wail as it moved toward her. A burst of frigid air encircled her body. "Noooo!"

"Hannah . . . Hannah . . ."

"Who are you?" she demanded. "What do you want?"

Behind her, she could hear the crackle of flames now. Yellow light flickered behind choking waves of black smoke from the open window.

Its fiery eyes glowing brighter, the shadow figure raised itself up, hovered closer, closer, stretching out its arms, preparing to pull her in.

23

Gripped with fear, Hannah raised her hands in front of her as if trying to shield herself.

She heard a sudden scrabbling at the window. A muffled cry above her head.

The shadow figure vanished.

And then she felt someone topple onto her.

They both fell in a heap to the ground.

"Alan!" she cried.

He struggled to his feet, his eyes wide with panic. "The matches!" he cried. "The matches! We — we didn't mean to. We — "

Another figure came diving out of the window as the crackle of flames grew to a roar. Fred landed hard on his elbows and knees.

Hannah stared at his dazed face in the darting orange light. "Fred — are you okay?"

"Danny," he muttered, gazing at her with horror. "Danny's in there. He can't get out."

"Huh?" Hannah leapt to her feet.

"Danny's trapped in the fire. He's going to burn!" Alan cried.

"We have to get help!" Fred said, shouting over the roar of the flames. He pulled Alan by the arm. The two boys took off, running unsteadily across the yard toward the house next door.

Bright orange-and-yellow flames licked at the windowsill above Hannah's head.

I have to save Danny, she thought.

She took a deep breath, gazing up at the flickering, flashing light of the fire. Then she started toward the open window.

But before she could take a step, the light from the window disappeared. The shadow rose in front of her.

"Hannah — go away." Its frightening, harsh whisper was so close to her face. "Go away."

"No!" Hannah screamed, forgetting her fear. "I have to save Danny."

"Hannah . . . you will not save him!" came the raspy reply.

The dark figure, eyes afire, hovered over her, blocking Hannah's path to the window.

"Let me go!" she screamed. "I have to save him!"

The red eyes loomed closer. The darkness fell heavier around her.

"Who *are* you?" Hannah shrieked. "*What* are you? What do you *want*?"

The dark figure didn't reply. The glowing eyes burned into hers.

Danny is trapped in there, Hannah thought. I *have* to get in that window.

"Move out of my way!" she screamed. And in her desperation, she reached out with both hands — grabbed the dark figure by the shoulders — and tried to shove it out of the way.

To Hannah's shock, the figure felt solid. With a determined cry, she raised her hands to its face — and tugged.

The darkness that cloaked its face fell away — and beneath the darkness, *Danny's face* was revealed!

24

Hannah stared in horror and disbelief, struggling to breathe. The sour odor choked her. The darkness continued to wrap around her, holding her prisoner.

Danny grinned back at her, with the same glowing red eyes as before he'd been unmasked.

"No!" Hannah cried, her voice a hoarse whisper, tight with fear. "It isn't you, Danny. It isn't!"

A cruel smile played over the figure's glowing face. "I am Danny's ghost!" he declared.

"Ghost?" Hannah tried to pull back. But the darkness held her tightly.

"I am Danny's ghost. When he dies in the fire, I will no longer be a shadow. I will be BORN — and Danny will go to the shadow world in my place!"

"No! No!" Hannah shrieked, raising her fists in

115

front of her. "No! Danny will not die! I won't let him!"

Danny's ghost opened its mouth and uttered a foul-smelling laugh. "You're too late, Hannah!" he sneered. "Too late."

25

"Nooooooo!"

Hannah's wail echoed in the darkness that surrounded her.

The ghost-Danny's red eyes flared angrily as Hannah burst right through him.

A second later, she was raising her hands to the window ledge. "Oh!" The sill was hot from the fire.

Using all her strength, she pulled herself up toward the darting flames — and into the house. A curtain of thick, sour smoke rose up to greet her.

Ignoring the smoke and the bright wall of fire, Hannah lowered herself heavily onto the floor.

I'm a ghost, she told herself, stepping into the blazing room.

I'm a ghost. I can't die again.

She rubbed her eyes with the sleeve of her T-shirt, struggling to see. "Danny?" she called, shouting as loudly as she could. "Danny — I can't see you! Where are you?"

Shielding her eyes with one hand, Hannah took another step into the room. Flames shot up like bright geysers. Wallpaper on one wall had curled down, the blackened corner covered with leaping flames.

"Danny — where are you?"

She heard a muffled shout from the next room. Dashing through the flame-encircled doorway, she saw him — trapped behind a tall wall of flames.

"Danny — !"

He was backed into a corner, his hands raised together in front of him, shielding his face from the smoke.

I can't get through those thick flames, Hannah realized to her horror.

She took another step into the room, then held back.

No way.

No way I can save him.

But once again, she reminded herself: *I am a ghost. I can do things that living people cannot do.*

"Help me! Help me!"

Danny's voice sounded tiny and far away behind the leaping waves of flame.

Without another second's hesitation, Hannah sucked in a deep breath, held it — and leapt into the flames.

"Help me!" He stared at her, his eyes blank. He didn't seem to see her. "Help!"

"Come on!" She grabbed his hand and tugged. "Let's go!"

The flames bent toward them, like fiery arms reaching to grab them.

"Come *on!*"

She tugged again, but he held back. "We can't make it!"

"Yes — we *have* to!" she shouted.

The heat burned her nostrils. She shut her eyes against the blinding yellow brightness. "We *have* to!"

She grabbed his hand with both of hers and pulled.

Black smoke swirled around them. Choking, she shut her eyes and pulled him, pulled him into the searing, blistering heat of the flames.

Into the flames.

Through them.

Coughing and choking. Dripping with perspiration from the furnacelike heat.

Pulled him. Pulled blindly. Pulled with all her might.

She didn't open her eyes until they were at the window.

She didn't breathe until they had tumbled to the cool darkness of the ground.

Then, on her hands and knees, panting so loudly, gasping for clean air, she gazed up.

There was the shadow figure near the house, twisting in flames. As the fire consumed it, it raised its dark arms toward the sky — and vanished without making a sound.

With a relieved sigh, Hannah lowered her gaze to Danny.

He was lying sprawled on his back, a dazed expression on his face. "Hannah," he whispered hoarsely. "Hannah, thanks."

She felt a smile start to cross her face.

Everything turned bright, as bright as the wall of flames.

Then everything went black.

26

Danny's mother leaned over him, pulling the light blanket up to his chest. "How are you feeling?" she asked softly.

It was two hours later. Danny had been treated by the paramedics who arrived shortly after the firefighters. They told his worried mother that he was suffering from smoke inhalation and had a few minor burns.

After treating the burns, they drove Danny and Mrs. Anderson home in an ambulance.

Now Danny lay in bed, staring up at her, still feeling groggy and dazed. Mrs. Quilty stood anxiously in the corner, her arms clasped tensely in front of her, looking on in silence. She had hurried over to see what the commotion was.

"I — I'm okay, I guess," Danny said, pulling himself up a bit on the pillow. "I'm just a little tired."

His mother pushed a lock of blond hair off her

forehead as she stared down at him, reading his lips. "How did you ever get out? How did you get out of the house?"

"It was Hannah," Danny told her. "Hannah pulled me out."

"Who?" Mrs. Anderson knotted her face in confusion. "Who is Hannah?"

"You know," Danny replied impatiently. "The girl next door."

"There's no girl next door," his mother said. "Is there, Molly?" She turned to read Mrs. Quilty's lips.

Mrs. Quilty shook her head. "The house is empty."

Danny sat up straight. "Her name is Hannah Fairchild. She saved my life, Mom."

Mrs. Quilty *tsk-tsked* sympathetically. "Hannah Fairchild is the girl who died five years ago," she said quietly. "Poor Danny is a bit delirious, I'm afraid."

"Just lie back," Danny's mother said, gently pushing him back onto the pillow. "Get some rest. You'll be fine."

"But where is Hannah? Hannah is my friend!" Danny insisted.

Hannah watched the scene from the doorway.

The three people in the room couldn't see her, she realized.

She had saved Danny's life, and now the room

and the people in it were growing faint, fading to gray.

Maybe that's why my family and I came back after five years, Hannah thought. Maybe we came back to save Danny from dying in a fire as we did.

"Hannah . . . Hannah . . ." A voice called to her. A sweet, familiar voice from far away.

"Is that you, Mom?" Hannah called.

"Time to come back," Mrs. Fairchild whispered. "You must leave now, Hannah. It's time to come back."

"Okay, Mom."

She gazed into the bedroom at Danny, lying peacefully on his pillow. He was fading away now, fading to gray.

Hannah squinted into the solid grayness. The house, she knew, was fading. The earth was fading from her sight.

"Come back, Hannah," her mother whispered. "Come back to us now."

Hannah could feel herself floating now. And as she floated, she gazed down — her last look at earth.

"I can see him, Mom," she said excitedly, brushing the tears off her cheeks. "I can see Danny. In his room. But the light is getting faint. So faint."

"Hannah, come back. Come back to us," her mother whispered, calling her home.

"Danny — remember me!" Hannah cried, as Danny's face appeared clearly in the misty gray.

Could he hear her?

Could he hear her calling to him?

She hoped so.

Add *more*

Goosebumps®

to your collection . . .

Here's a chilling preview of

THE HAUNTED MASK

7

Carly Beth sighed and peered in through the glass. The walls of the tiny store were covered with masks. The masks seemed to stare back at her.

They're laughing at me, she thought unhappily. Laughing at me because I'm too late. Because the store is closed, and I'm going to have to be a stupid duck for Halloween.

Suddenly, a dark shadow moved over the glass, blocking Carly Beth's view. She gasped and took a step back.

It took her a moment to realize that the shadow was a man. A man in a black suit, staring out at her, a look of surprise on his face.

"Are you — are you closed?" Carly Beth shouted through the glass.

The man gestured that he couldn't hear her. He turned the lock and pulled the door open an inch. "May I help you?" he asked curtly. He had shiny black hair, parted in the middle and slicked down on his head, and a pencil-thin black mustache.

"Are you open?" Carly Beth asked timidly. "I need a Halloween mask."

"It's very late," the man replied, not answering her question. He pulled the door open another few inches. "We normally close at five."

"I really would like to buy a mask," Carly Beth told him in her most determined voice.

The man's tiny, black eyes peered into hers. His expression remained blank. "Come in," he said quietly.

As Carly Beth stepped past him into the store, she saw that he wore a black cape. It must be a Halloween costume, she told herself. I'm sure he doesn't wear that all the time.

She turned her attention to the masks on the two walls.

"What kind of mask are you looking for?" the man asked, closing the door behind him.

Carly Beth felt a stab of fear. His black eyes glowed like two burning coals. He seemed so strange. And here she was, locked in this closed store with him.

"A s-scary one," she stammered.

He rubbed his chin thoughtfully. He pointed to the wall. "The gorilla mask has been very popular. It has real hair. I believe I may have one left in stock."

Carly Beth stared up at the gorilla mask. She didn't really want to be a gorilla. It was too ordinary. It wasn't scary enough. "Hmmm . . . do you have anything scarier?" she asked.

He flipped his cape back over the shoulder of his black suit. "How about that yellowish one with the pointy ears?" he suggested, pointing. "I believe it's some sort of *Star Trek* character. I still have a few of them, I believe."

"No." Carly Beth shook her head. "I need something really scary."

A strange smile formed under the man's thin mustache. His eyes burned into hers, as if trying to read her thoughts. "Look around," he said, with a sweep of his hand. "Everything I have left in stock is up on the walls."

Carly Beth turned her gaze to the masks. A pig mask with long, ugly tusks and blood trickling from the snout caught her eye. Pretty good, she thought. But not quite right.

A hairy werewolf mask with white, pointy fangs was hung beside it. Again, too ordinary, Carly Beth decided.

Her eyes glanced over a green Frankenstein mask, a Freddy Krueger mask that came with Freddy's hand — complete with long, silvery blades for fingers — and an E.T. mask.

Just not scary enough, Carly Beth thought, starting to feel a little desperate. I need something that will really make Steve and Chuck die of fright!

"Young lady, I am afraid I must ask you to make

your choice," the man in the cape said softly. He had moved behind the narrow counter at the front and was turning a key in the cash register. "We really are closed, after all."

"I'm sorry," Carly Beth started. "It's just that — "

The phone rang before she could finish explaining.

The man picked it up quickly and began talking in a low voice, turning his back to Carly Beth.

She wandered toward the back of the store, studying the masks as she walked. She passed a black cat mask with long, ugly yellow fangs. A vampire mask with bright red blood trickling down its lips was hung next to a grinning, bald mask of Uncle Fester from *The Addams Family*.

Not right, not right, not right, Carly Beth thought, frowning.

She hesitated when she spotted a narrow door slightly opened at the back of the store. Was there another room? Were there more masks back there?

She glanced to the front. The man, hidden behind his cape, still had his back to her as he talked on the phone.

Carly Beth gave the door a hesitant push to peek inside. The door creaked open. Pale orange light washed over the small, shadowy back room.

Carly Beth stepped inside — and gasped in amazement.

8

Two dozen empty eye sockets stared blindly at Carly Beth.

She gaped in horror at the distorted, deformed faces.

They were masks, she realized. Two shelves of masks. But the masks were so ugly, so grotesque — so *real* — they made her breath catch in her throat.

Carly Beth gripped the doorframe, reluctant to enter the tiny back room. Staring into the dim orange light, she studied the hideous masks.

One mask had long, stringy yellow hair falling over its bulging, green forehead. A hairy black rat's head poked up from a knot in the hair, the rat's eyes gleaming like two dark jewels.

The mask beside it had a large nail stuck through an eyehole. Thick, wet-looking blood poured from the eye, down the cheek.

Chunks of rotting skin appeared to be falling off another mask, revealing gray bone underneath. An enormous black insect, some kind of grotesque beetle, poked out from between the green-and-yellow decayed teeth.

Carly Beth's horror mixed with excitement. She took a step into the room. The wooden floorboards creaked noisily beneath her.

She took another step closer to the grotesque, grinning masks. They seemed so real, so horribly real. The faces had such detail. The skin appeared to be made of flesh, not rubber or plastic.

These are perfect! she thought, her heart pounding. These are just what I was looking for. They look *terrifying* just propped up on these shelves!

She imagined Steve and Chuck seeing one of these masks coming at them in the dark of night. She pictured herself uttering a bloodcurdling scream and leaping out from behind a tree in one of them.

She imagined the horrified expressions on the boys' faces. She pictured Steve and Chuck shrieking in terror and running for their lives.

Perfect. Perfect!

What a laugh that would be. What a victory!

Carly Beth took a deep breath and stepped up to the shelves. Her eyes settled on an ugly mask on the lower shelf.

It had a bulging, bald head. Its skin was a putrid yellow-green. Its enormous, sunken eyes were an eerie orange and seemed to glow. It had a broad, flat nose, smashed in like a skeleton's nose. The dark-lipped mouth gaped wide, revealing jagged animal fangs.

Staring hard at the hideous mask, Carly Beth reached out a hand toward it. Reluctantly, she touched the broad forehead.

And as she touched it, the mask cried out.

About the Author

R.L. STINE is the author of the series *Fear Street*, *Nightmare Room*, *Give Yourself Goosebumps*, and the phenomenally successful *Goosebumps*. His thrilling teen titles have sold more than 250 million copies internationally — enough to earn him a spot in the *Guinness Book of World Records*! Mr. Stine lives in New York City with his wife, Jane, and his son, Matt.

YOU'VE READ THE BOOKS...
NOW OWN THE THRILLS ON DVD

BRING HOME THE EXCITEMENT!

**R.L. Stine Classics
Come To DVD
For The First Time
From Twentieth Century
Fox Home Entertainment!**

www.foxhome.com

SCHOLASTIC

www.scholastic.com/

Collect Them All!

Goosebumps®

By R.L. Stine

Each Book $4.99

- ❑ Goosebumps: Abominable Snowman of Pasadena
- ❑ Goosebumps: Attack of the Jack-O-Lanterns
- ❑ Goosebumps: Attack of The Mutant
- ❑ Goosebumps: Bad Hare Day
- ❑ Goosebumps: Barking Ghost
- ❑ Goosebumps: The Beast from the East
- ❑ Goosebumps: Be Careful What You Wish For...
- ❑ Goosebumps: The Cuckoo Clock of Doom
- ❑ Goosebumps: The Curse of Camp Cold Lake
- ❑ Goosebumps: Curse of the Mummy's Tomb
- ❑ Goosebumps: Deep Trouble
- ❑ Goosebumps: Egg Monsters from Mars
- ❑ Goosebumps: Ghost Beach
- ❑ Goosebumps: Ghost Camp
- ❑ Goosebumps: Ghost Next Door
- ❑ Goosebumps: The Girl Who Cried Monster
- ❑ Goosebumps: Go Eat Worms!
- ❑ Goosebumps: The Haunted Mask
- ❑ Goosebumps: The Haunted Mask II
- ❑ Goosebumps: The Headless Ghost
- ❑ Goosebumps: The Horror at Camp Jellyjam
- ❑ Goosebumps: How I Got My Shrunken Head
- ❑ Goosebumps: How to Kill a Monster
- ❑ Goosebumps: It Came from Beneath the Sink!
- ❑ Goosebumps: Lets Get Invisible
- ❑ Goosebumps: Monster Blood
- ❑ Goosebumps: Monster Blood II
- ❑ Goosebumps: A Night in Terror Tower
- ❑ Goosebumps: Night of the Living Dummy
- ❑ Goosebumps: Night of the Living Dummy II
- ❑ Goosebumps: Night of the Living Dummy III
- ❑ Goosebumps: One Day at HorrorLand
- ❑ Goosebumps: Piano Lessons Can Be Murder
- ❑ Goosebumps: Revenge of the Lawn Gnomes
- ❑ Goosebumps: Say Cheese and Die!
- ❑ Goosebumps: Say Cheese and Die — Again!
- ❑ Goosebumps: The Scarecrow Walks at Midnight
- ❑ Goosebumps: Shocker on Shock Street
- ❑ Goosebumps: Stay Out of the Basement
- ❑ Goosebumps: Vampire Breath
- ❑ Goosebumps: Welcome to Camp Nightmare
- ❑ Goosebumps: Welcome to Dead House
- ❑ Goosebumps: The Werewolf of Fever Swamp
- ❑ Goosebumps: Why I'm Afraid of Bees
- ❑ Goosebumps: You Can't Scare Me!

■ SCHOLASTIC

Read at Your Own Risk
Goosebumps

By R. L. Stine

Each Book $4.99

____ 0-439-72705-8 Goosebumps: Attack of the Jack-O-Lanterns

____ 0-439-66215-X Goosebumps: Attack of The Mutant

____ 0-439-66216-8 Goosebumps: Bad Hare Day

____ 0-439-66990-1 Goosebumps: Be Careful What You Wish For

____ 0-439-72403-1 Goosebumps: The Beast from the East

____ 0-439-72404-X Goosebumps: The Curse of Camp Cold Lake

____ 0-439-56828-5 Goosebumps: Deep Trouble

____ 0-439-56829-3 Goosebumps: Egg Monsters from Mars

____ 0-439-56830-7 Goosebumps: Ghost Beach

____ 0-439-56831-5 Goosebumps: Ghost Camp

____ 0-439-69353-5 Goosebumps: The Girl Who Cried Monster

____ 0-439-67114-0 Goosebumps: Go Eat Worms!

____ 0-439-67113-2 Goosebumps: The Haunted Mask II

____ 0-439-66987-1 Goosebumps: The Headless Ghost

____ 0-439-56837-4 Goosebumps: It Came from Beneath the Sink!

____ 0-439-66988-X Goosebumps: Monster Blood II

____ 0-439-67111-6 Goosebumps: A Night in Terror Tower

____ 0-439-57374-2 Goosebumps: Night of the Living Dummy II

____ 0-439-66989-8 Goosebumps: Night of the Living Dummy III

____ 0-439-56841-2 Goosebumps: One Day at HorrorLand

____ 0-439-67112-4 Goosebumps: Piano Lessons Can Be Murder

____ 0-439-57375-0 Goosebumps: Revenge of the Lawn Gnomes

____ 0-439-56842-0 Goosebumps: Say Cheese and Die!

____ 0-439-57361-0 Goosebumps: Say Cheese and Die—Again!

____ 0-439-56843-9 Goosebumps: The Scarecrow Walks at Midnight

____ 0-439-72706-6 Goosebumps: Vampire Breath

____ 0-439-56846-3 Goosebumps: Welcome to Camp Nightmare

____ 0-439-56848-X Goosebumps: The Werewolf of Fever Swamp

____ 0-439-57365-3 Goosebumps: You Can't Scare Me!

____ 0-439-69354-3 Goosebumps: Why Im Afraid of Bees

Available Wherever Books Are Sold, or Use This Order Form.

Scholastic Inc., P.O. Box 7502, Jefferson City, MO 65102

Please send me the books I have checked above. I am enclosing $_____ (please add $2.00 to cover shipping and handling). Send check or money order—no cash or C.O.D.s please.

Name_____ Birth date_____

Address_____

City_____ State/Zip_____

Please allow four to six weeks for delivery. Offer good in U.S.A. only. Sorry, mail orders are not available to residents of Canada. Prices subject to change.

■SCHOLASTIC

GBC0805